James Lawson

The Maiden's Oath

A Domestic Drama

James Lawson

The Maiden's Oath
A Domestic Drama

ISBN/EAN: 9783337342494

Printed in Europe, USA, Canada, Australia, Japan

Cover: Foto ©Andreas Hilbeck / pixelio.de

More available books at **www.hansebooks.com**

THE MAIDEN'S OATH

A DOMESTIC DRAMA

————————

YONKERS
1877

DRAMATIS PERSONÆ.

--- ----+ ++--- --- ---

RIVERS, OF WEELOUNDELL,	*A Gentleman Farmer.*
WILDER,	*A near Neighbor.*
EDWARD CARRYL,	*In love with Mary Rivers.*
CHARLES WATERS, .	*Mrs. Wilder's Cousin.*
FOUNTAIN,	*A Wall-Street Broker.*
GREENLAKE,.	*A Farmer.*
VAN SNAP,	*A Country Lawyer.*
JAKE,	*A Black Boy.*
MRS. RIVERS.	
MRS. WILDER.	
MARY RIVERS.	

Farmers, Footmen, Chambermaids, Servants, etc.

Scene on the Hudson.

Time : A Week in June.

THE MAIDEN'S OATH.

ACT I.

Scene I.—A Parlor at Weeloundell.

Mr. *and* Mrs. Rivers, *seated.*

Mrs. R. Well, husband, read the letter once again.

Rivers. [*Reads.*]

> "It was my good fortune to meet Miss Rivers during her late visit to the city, and in her society I spent many pleasant hours. With the approbation of Mrs. Plume (whose note, the warrant for my intrusion, I enclose) I take the liberty of confessing that it would afford me, with your kind permission, much pleasure to visit Weeloundell. Please present my compliments to Miss Rivers, and believe me, with much respect,
> > "Your obedient servant,
> > > "Edward Carryl."

Rivers. He writes a graceful hand.

Mrs. R. [*Sighing.*] Polite and civil.

Rivers. A smile would more become you than a sigh.

Mrs. R. This, the first moment that I realize
Our dear, sweet girl has passed her infant days ;
Perhaps is loved, perhaps the love returns.

Rivers. What answer shall we send ? .

Mrs. R. [*Thoughtfully.*]   But yesterday
 She was a child ; to-day the sudden thought
 She is a woman, flashes on my mind,
 And I must needs admit it for a truth.
 How swiftly glide the happy years away !

Rivers.   Why are you sad ?   Be thankful she is spared,
 A truthful girl, the comfort of our home.

Mrs. R. [*Musing.*]   Love wins its way into the sin-
  less heart,
 Like dreams which unaware intrude on sleep,
 And gathering strength, ere judgment is awake,
 It rules the wisest with a power supreme.

Rivers.   Shall we invite him ?

Mrs. R.   Give me time to think.
 Why did not cousin bring him up herself ?

Rivers.   No doubt the latest fashion—just imported.

Mrs. R.   She spoke of many gentlemen she saw,
 But not once mentioned him : is it not strange ?

Rivers.   No—if she loves.

Mrs. R.   He must be well connected,
 Else cousin had not recommended him.

Rivers.   She is a prudent, a discerning woman ;
 And doubtless knows he is a man of merit.

Mrs. R.   But simple merit, in this gaudy world,
 Is comfortless and cold.

Rivers.   In fashion's creed.
 Give me an honest, intellectual man,
 One who, in homely phrase, is well to do,

And I shall like him : what care I for fops,
Or fools who prate of what you call—position.

Mrs. R. I do not know a family of the name.

Rivers. Is that a valid argument against him ?
Thousands ne'er heard of us, nor Weeloundell ;
Are we less worthy in our own esteem,
Or undervalued by a soul who knows us ?
The true man needs no ostentatious aids
To prove his innate honesty and worth.

Mrs. R. I do not comprehend your vulgar notions.

Rivers. We never do agree.   [*Rising to go.*

Mrs. R. Sit down and listen.

Rivers. Take your own course, exactly as you please.

Mrs. R. Two ways to do a thing, the wrong and right ;
You somehow always stumble on the wrong.

Rivers. So much to do I have not time to argue.

Mrs. R. Hurry is your hobby—sit down, I say.
                         [*Rivers resumes his seat.*
Yet, after all, this may be fancy merely—
A kindly feeling, not a softer passion.

Rivers. A civil note deserves a prompt reply.

Mrs. R. He must have means, a business or profession,
He would not else aspire to Mary's hand.

Rivers. You jump unwisely to a rash conclusion.

Mrs. R. He may not visit in the highest circles.

Rivers. Well, if he don't—any the worse for that ?

Mrs. R. Would Cousin Plume have sanctioned such a
   letter,

Unless he had confessed more than he writes?
Be cautious, act with dignified reserve,
Not vulgar haste.

Rivers. Again I tell you, wife,
I sympathize not with your lofty notions,
And never did.   Truth, clad in homespun, wins
· Sincerer friends than silken falsehood claims.

Mrs. R. A trite old maxim, thrust in, head and heels.

Rivers. Mistake not rich apparel for refinement,
Nor graceful manner for an upright heart.

> [*Enter* JAKE: *a huge silver watch in his fob:*
> *a flashy ribbon outside, from which sundry*
> *baubles dangle.*

Mrs. R. Why this giggling?

Jake. Me! Dunno, missus, shuah.
Guess massa like we look jes sah.

Rivers. Silence!

Mrs. R. What is the matter?

Rivers. Out with it.

Jake. Yees, massa.   [*Takes out his watch.*
Dis watch say, missus—jes 'leven de clock, shuah.
An' Massa Wilda's carriage jes driv' up.

Mrs. R. For once be serious, Jake, or I shall scold.
Bid him walk in.   [*Exit* JAKE.

Rivers. You spoil the foolish boy
By too much freedom, and that silver watch,
Your Christmas gift, has turned his woolly pate.
He grows in nothing save in idleness.

Mrs. R. Put up the letter.

        [*Enter* WILDER.

Wilder. Valued friends, good morning.

    Do I intrude ?

Mrs. R. Oh no, sir—always welcome.

Wilder. [*Taking Mr. Rivers' hand.*]

    I gladly take your hand ; how fresh you look.

    Time, on your brow, sits lightly ; you wear well.

Rivers. None forty years ago observed my looks.

    What news ?

Wilder. None sir, save, on my annual tour,

    I come soliciting for foreign Missions :

    How much shall I put down as your subscription ?

Rivers. I will not give one cent to foreign lands,

    When heathen swarm around our very door. [times.

Wilder. [*Aside.*] That has been meanly urged a thousand

    [*To him.*] Sorry a man, so kind and generous,

    Refuses aid to this deserving cause—

    The cause which civilizes pagan lands,

    And teaches man to love his fellow man—

    To offer praise and thankfulness to Him,

    Source of each blessing here, and hope hereafter.

Rivers. Preach as you please, but let me tell you

        frankly,

    Some for self-glory beg, not pious zeal ;

    And, to get rid of tedious, canting fools,

    The busy business man oft freely gives,

    While vanity subscribes with open hand

To see his name paraded in the papers.

Wilder. Yet let me add, some, with a heart devout,
    Contribute largely.

Rivers. [*Roughly.*] Each one to his taste.

Wilder. Sir, I must take my leave : madam, adieu.
    Pity that good men scoff at works of grace. [*Exit.*

Mrs. R. You have offended that religious man.

Rivers. I cannot give to every one who asks.

Mrs. R. Give each a little and assist them all.

Rivers. Am I to shape my givings in his mould ?
    You know me liberal, not as zealots plead,
    But as my own benevolence approves,
    To lessen crime and poverty at home.

Mrs. R. I am ashamed and mortified to death.
    What will the people say ?

Rivers. Just what they please :
    Why, what care I for moths and butterflies ?

                    [*Re-enter* WILDER.

Wilder. I beg your pardon—I forgot to ask,
    How is my favorite, your fair daughter, madam ?

Mrs. R. Quite well.

Wilder. She spent a pleasant time in town ?

Mrs. R. Delighted with her visit, she returned,
    And is most welcome back : her absence proved
    A house is cheerless when its light is gone.

Wilder. Young Waters tells me she was much admired :
    He came last night to spend a week with us.

Mrs. R. We shall be glad to see him with your wife—

At any time ; always at home to her.
Husband, our friend may know the gentleman.
We have received a note from Edward Carryl,
On—no matter now—some business of his own ;
Sir, do you know him ?

Wilder. Yes—I knew him once ;
Three years at Princeton we were college mates :
He was a student then—a close one too.
Some think him cold, morose, but I believe
(Tho' men censorious falter in his praise)
That in the classics he finds truer pleasure
Than truant youths in their unblest conceits.

Mrs. R. What is his business, sir ?

Wilder. He studied law :
Of late, we seldom meet ; yet I have heard
He more delights in Bryant than in Kent,
And while young lawyers strive in court, to win
Fortune and fame, he in the closet sits
Wooing the muses.

Rivers. Fantastic beggars,
Whom you may meet in every lane or alley,
And numerous as mosquitos in the swamp.

Wilder. That matters not to him.

Mrs. R. How ! Is he rich ?

Wilder. Perhaps not rich in these luxurious times,
But rich enough, they say, to live at ease.

Rivers. That is sufficient ; if he more desires,
Let him consult his heart and not his purse.

9*

Mrs. R. A man of culture and a poet too !

Wilder. I think he writes for pastime, not for fame.

Mrs. R. Contributes to the monthly magazines ?

Wilder. There the young poet tries his earliest flight.

Rivers. Or poet's corner in the county paper.

Mrs. R. Does he write well ?

Wilder. Not having read his lines,

To censure were unkind, to praise, unjust.

Rivers. I hope he is too sensible a man

To waste his time in scribbling useless rhymes.

Wilder. Madam, perhaps you know not Edward Carryl—

Met he Miss Rivers when she was in town ?

Whate'er his business, sir—purchase or sale ?

Believe me, he, in merchant phrase, is " good."

Mrs. R. The value of your counsel we have proved,

Else we should not have troubled you with this.

We scarce know what to say ; but, if need be,

We yet may trespass on your kind advice.

Wilder. Good morning, madam.   I shall give my wife

Your courteous invitation.

       [*Going and aside.*]   My wits must work.

To find what Carryl wants ; if he come here,

Rage and revenge awake !   [*Exit.*

Rivers. What say you now ?

You often praise his unobtrusive manners,

And hold him up a pattern for the world.

Mrs. R. And so I do : I wish you were his like.

Rivers. Eager to learn what you refused to tell,

He gazed into your eye to read it there.

Mrs. R. Was I not right to keep the matter secret?

Rivers. Surely—a thousand reasons why you should,
　　Not one why he should ask, or hint to know;
　　And yet he did. What could his object be?

Mrs. R. Interest in us.

Rivers. No—curiosity,
　　Or, were truth told, perhaps a baser motive.

Mrs. R. I wish you would think kindly of my friend.

Rivers. In my opinion he is cold and crafty.

Mrs. R. Oh, no; a pious, charitable man,
　　And in his smile, something—I know not what,
　　Wins my esteem.

Rivers. Oh! very sweet and bland
　　Which is perfection in a woman's eye;
　　But I prefer stern morals to soft manners.

Mrs. R. Who ever heard a word against his morals?
　　A faithful husband, an obliging neighbor,
　　Modest, urbane, an honest, godly man;
　　The world may trust him with uncounted gold.

Rivers. I do not like his looks.

Mrs. R. Is that his fault?

Rivers. Retort, that's right, retort; but to the letter.

Mrs. R. No need of haste; first, let me question Mary,
　　Then we may send him a discreet reply.　[*Exeunt.*

Scene II.—*The Garden.* Mary Rivers *busy*
among the flowers.

Mary. 'Tis now a month since I returned from town,
And not a line received from Cousin Plume,
Nor other friends.   I sometimes think of them;
I wonder if they waste a thought on us !
So much to do, so many calls to make,
Such sights to see, and shopping to be done—
If not to purchase, yet to see the fashions—
I should not blame them if we are forgotten.
He often praised the charms of country life
Above the din and bustle of the town,
And wished, he said, he had been bred a farmer—
Fancy, perhaps, or courtesy to me :
But it would please me if, perchance, he came
To spend a day with us at Weeloundell—
Not that I care especially for him ;
Only to show him father's taste and skill,
And my sweet flowers ; he surely would admire them.
How well he talks !   Always some news to tell,
Or interesting story to relate :
And when he reads, how musical his voice !
Oh ! I could listen all the summer day,
And never tire !
            [*Enter* Mrs. Rivers.
Mrs. R. Still busy in the garden ?
      You are too much exposed; the sun is warm.

Mary. Yes, very warm.

Mrs. R. Where is your parasol ?

Mary. I need both hands to cultivate my flowers.

Mrs. R. And where your sun hat ?

Mary. This I wear must do.

Mrs. R. You will be tanned brown as a nut ere fall.

　I have not seen this neat parterre before.

Mary. You like it ?

Mrs. R. Very gracefully arranged.

Mary. All is the gardener's work, but mine the plan.

Mrs. R. Since you returned ? What do you call this

　flower ?　　　　　　　　　　　　　　　[tion ?

Mary. Mother, you know : how can you ask the ques-

　Scarlet geranium in a crescent bed.

Mrs. R. Crescent ! it looks more like the letter C.

Mary. Oh, no ! you surely do not see aright.

Mrs. R. And what is that ?

Mary. The sweet verbena, mother.

Mrs. R. It also looks exactly like a C.

Mary. [*Confused.*] Whose carriage came just now ?

Mrs. R. Good Mr. Wilder's.

　Are all your beds made in this singular shape ?

Mary. Oh, no ; this, square ; that, oval ; here, a diamond ;

　Another round, yonder an octagon—

　An infinite variety of shapes.

Mrs. R. But in those crescents, as you chose to call

　I see your favorite flowers.　　　　　　　[them,

Mary. O mother, no !

I have no special favorites ; all I love—
All in their season.   Why did Wilder call ?

Mrs. R. Only to see your father ; and he said
That Charles Waters——

Mary. Tell me, what of him ?

Mrs. R. Arrived last night.

Mary. Sure, I am very glad,
For he will give us all the city news.
Does any talk of coming up to see us ?

Mrs. R. The fashion is to leave the town in June.
Waters you must have seen at Cousin Plume's.

Mary. Yes, frequently we met.

Mrs. R. Who else, my child ?

Mary. I made acquaintance with a dozen girls.

Mrs. R. With gentlemen, of course ?

Mary. Twenty at least ;
At balls and theatres as many more.

Mrs. R. With some you were more intimate than others.
We all have favorites, doubtless you have yours ;
If you had not, it would indeed be strange.

Mary. None in particular—I acknowledge none.

Mrs. R. Not one whom you desire to see again ?

Mary. O mother, yes ! They were so very civil,
I should be glad to see them once again,
And hope I shall, next winter, in the city.

Mrs. R. Was any one a little more than civil ?

Mary. I do not at this moment think there was.

Mrs. R. These sweet geraniums take the shape of C.

You call them crescents—the verbenas too,

A similar form ; my child, why do you blush ?

What thought suggested those peculiar figures ?

Mary. Do you admire them ?

Mrs. R. Yes, indeed I do.

A magic in this crescent, as you called it.

Is it a feeling, Mary, or a fancy ?

Mary. Dear mother ! I have nothing to conceal ;

You know it, mother, yet you press me strangely—

I cannot tell, it must be accidental.

Is rumor busy ? I am not to blame

For every look or word that passed between us

Politeness would approve.

Mrs. R. Impulsive girl !

Whoe'er he is, he has a champion here.

Mary. What said I, mother, nothing, sure, amiss

To shield the absent ?

Mrs. R. I have not accused.

It seems but yesterday you were a child,

The world has changed, you are a woman now ;

And, at your age, as natural to love

As flowers are to the spring ; guard well your heart,

For oft the artful flatterer succeeds

Where modest merit fails.

Mary. A purer man,

One more sincere, breathes not than Edward Carryl.

Ask Cousin Plume, write her this very hour;

She, with additions, will confirm my words.

Mrs. R. Who is this Carryl you defend so warmly ?

Mary. He never thought of me, nor I of him—
 Oh ! very sure—save in a social way.

Mrs. R. But who is he ?

Mary. A general favorite ;
 No kinder welcome gave I than the rest.

[Enter RIVERS.

Rivers. What say you, wife ?

Mrs. R. You may invite him, husband.

Mary. You taught me never to conceal a thought,
 I never did : invite him ! tell me, who ?

Mrs. R. Give her the letter.

[RIVERS gives MARY the letter.
Look ; observe that blush ;

 A tender passion nestles in her heart
 Of which she little dreams.   May he prove true,
 And worthy her.

Rivers. What answer shall we send ?

Mary. [*Much embarrassed.*] Methinks 'tis very warm ;
  the air is close,
 Sultry, and damp—but growing weather, father.

Rivers. Shall we invite him, child ?

Mary. Mother says, yes.

Rivers. And shall I any message send from you ?

Mary. It threatens rain ; the fields are dry and parched ;
 We need some rain ; a shower would help the crops.

Mrs. R. Let us not crowd on her embarrassment,
 It will soon pass.

Rivers. Give me the letter, daughter.

[MARY *returns it abstractedly.*

Mrs. R. Come straight in-doors; this note we shall
    consider.

Now leave the garden, while you court the shade ;

The flowers, tho' you are absent, will not fade.

[*Exeunt.*

SCENE III.—WILDER'S *Library.*

Enter MRS. WILDER *and* WATERS.

Mrs. W. [*Laughing.*] Now, Cousin Waters, tell the
    blessed truth,

Confess for once your callous heart is touched ;

I know it, sir ; 'tis needless to deny.

Waters. May not a man admire a pretty face

With heart unwounded ?

Mrs. W. Yes, if it be stone ;

But yours is veritable flesh and blood,

Tho'—let me whisper, cousin—very soft.

Waters. More women laugh aloud than think aright.

Mrs. W. There, sage philosopher, we both agree.

But, cousin dear, pray do not take offence ;

You are the gentlest man if not the wisest.

Waters. How can you laugh ? do I provoke your mirth?

Mrs. W. Oh, no, most learned judge of—maiden charms !

Waters. Miss Rivers is indeed a lovely girl ;

Troops of admirers, while at Mrs. Plume's,

   Besieged her heart, yet still she lived unspoiled.

Mrs. W. And made some conquests too ?

Waters. Some, cousin, some !

   Her unobtrusive sprightliness and grace

   Secured the triumphs which her beauty won.

Mrs. W. Does sober judgment praise a creature thus ?

   In scale humane all are of equal weight,

   But man's wild fancy in one damsel sees

   Charms that surpass the rest of womankind

   (That is when he puts on love's spectacles)

   Which, calm observers never could discover.

   Yet I admit she is an excellent girl,

   Comely, accomplished, and a good musician ;

   I think that she would rather sacrifice

   Her love, yea life itself, than falsely speak.

Waters. She is the purest, fairest in the land !

Mrs. W. Alack, dear Waters, you are deep in love :

   Well, well, poor man, husband and I will help.

   You may depend on us.

Waters.   Is love a trade,

   That by commission we may carry on,

   And bring to profitable market ?

Mrs. W. Why not ?

Waters. Heart must with heart accord, and eye with eye

   Exchange fond looks, more eloquent than words ;

   A feeling dwells in every human breast,

   Deeper than thought, as precious as our breath,

   Which needs no intercessor ; if not there

Beating with mutual bound, what would avail
Pleading or promise of a generous friend ?

Mrs. W. Have you lighted !   Waters, how old are you ?

Waters. Why ask ? You know that I am twenty-four.

Mrs. W. Bless me ! so very old, and yet so foolish !
You rave as wildly as a beardless boy.
Your silly pate ne'er hatched a speech so fine,
You must have learned it from some tragic play.
Pity your father left his only son
So much more wealth than wit !

Waters. Unsparing cousin,
How you delight to tantalize and laugh !

Mrs. W. Mirth is the sweetest tune, care killed the cat ;
You may be sure it never will kill me.

Waters. A tune, tho' sweet, too oft repeated, tires.

Mrs. W. What ! tired of me ! Go right back to the city,
For not one word shall I speak in your favor.

Waters. Will you be serious, for one moment listen ?

Mrs. W. No ! hold your peace : but had you better
    manners
You might have gone with me to Weeloundell ;
Now, not a step.

Waters. Have I offended you ?

Mrs. W. Oh ! you have missed a famous opportunity
To learn the country is a social place,
Not selfish like the city ; there, I am told,
Your next-door neighbor may fall sick or die,
Marry or break, and not a soul the wiser ;

But here, neighbor is neighbor miles around,
And sympathizes with a lively feeling
In all our hopes and fears ; but you, wise man,
Of this know just as much as I of Greek.
Now do not answer, 'tis no earthly use,
For your town ignorance is no excuse.

Waters. What look you for, from me ?

Mrs. W. From you, sir—nothing !
  Tho', had you brains enough to serve a sparrow—
  Now don't be angry, coz—you might have found
  Each with the other strives for warmest welcome.

Waters. As welcome as the latest novel, coz,
  To cheer the humdrum of a country life.

Mrs. W. A monstrous libel !   Learn a hundred years,
  You may be wise—not sooner, by my troth.

          [*Enter* WILDER.

Waters. Right glad you have returned.

Mrs. W. And so am I.
  Do tell the sighing youth, is Mary well ?

Waters. Cousin, they say, you are at times sarcastic.

Mrs. W. They say—O ! excellent authority !

Wilder. What means this banter ?

Mrs. W. Waters is in love.

Wilder. In love ! in love with whom ?   With you or me ?

Mrs. W. Oh, no, no, no !   With Mary Rivers, husband.

Waters. I have not told you so.   Your teasing wife,
  Plagued with inventive fits, finds ample mirth
  In vain imaginings.

Mrs. W. A weak evasion :

 If he is not, never was man in love ;

 Believe me, dear.

Wilder. He has no time to lose.

Mrs. W. Hey-day ! a rival ?   That is news indeed.

 Who is he ? tell me ; handsome, wise, or rich ?

Wilder. I am not sure, and shall not tell my guess.

Mrs. W. Poor, stricken deer ! husband and I will help.

 Droop not, nor pine, for we are famous pleaders.

Wilder. Madam invites you both to Weeloundell.

Mrs. W. Unharness not the horses ; in an hour

 I shall be ready.   Make your toilet, cousin,

 Prink to the best ; detain him not, dear husband ;

 For, as you say, he has no time to lose.   [*Exit.*

Wilder. What fancy does my wayward wife pursue ?

Waters. I praised Miss Rivers, and she thence infers

 More than I said.

Wilder. You know the damsel, then ?

Waters. We met at Mrs. Plume's.

Wilder. And much admired ?

Waters. She was indeed.

Wilder. Who seemed to please her most ?

Waters. Courteous to all, we thought she favored none,

 None in particular.

Wilder. Met she Carryl there ?

Waters. Very often.

Wilder. Were his attentions marked ?

Waters. Yes, so devoted,

By all, except herself, they were observed.

Wilder. Indeed ! one question more : love you Miss
   Rivers ?

Waters. The hope of meeting her, I may confess,
  Hastened my visit.

Wilder. That is quite enough.
  As kinsman of my wife, as friend to me,
  I know my duty ; and, in your behalf,
  Shall use my power : besides, I owe you thanks,
  For, when enticed to speculate in stocks,
  Your purse and credit were at my command,
  Which I appreciate ; and your generous loans,
  More richly than in coin, I may requite.
  Our friends have faith in me.

Waters. I thank you, Wilder.

Wilder. A rival I suspect stands in your path ;
  His chance to win her, more or less than yours,
  I do not know. Guess you the man ? 'Tis Carryl.
  We soon may see him ; he perhaps will find
  My neighborhood is not a pleasant place
  For him to visit.

Waters. You would not do him harm ?

Wilder. He never shall be Rivers' son-in-law.
  I say no more ; but breathe not this aloud,
  Else you may frustrate my well-meant designs.

Waters. By disappointing him you favor me.

Wilder. To you devoted, heart and hand : now go.
        [*Exit* WATERS.

Forget me, Heaven ! if ever I forgive
His venomed malice—some misnamed, his truth—
Which blazed my indiscretions to the world,
And forced me in disgrace to leave the college.
Never left word unsaid, nor act undone,
To slur my name and mortify my pride :
What cause had he ?   The devil in his heart
That gloried in my shame.   I know not much ;
But this for certain know, I hate the wretch.
I keep, securely keep, an Indian book
In which, with blood-red ink, I write my wrongs,
And never cancel till discharged in full.
The infernal gods, who nourish mortal wrath,
Tho' waiting long and seeming to forgive,
In patience wait for sure and safe revenge,
But not in vain : now chance seems opportune
To feast my soul with exquisite content,
But wit and guile must lead me to success.

[*Exit.*

ACT II.

SCENE. I—*The Piazza at Weeloundell.*

MRS. RIVERS *knitting.   Enter* RIVERS *from the house.*

Mrs. R. What is the hurry ?

Rivers. I have work to do.

Mrs. R. What work ?

Rivers. To-day the buckwheat must be sown.

Mrs. R. Plenty of time for that a fortnight hence ;
    Now, stop a moment.

Rivers. Well, what do you want ?

Mrs. R. Only to ask—how like you Edward Carryl ?
    With ample opportunities to judge,
    You must by this time have made up your mind ;
    Then tell me calmly what you think of him.

Rivers. A well-bred, modest man, in my opinion ;
    Besides, he takes an interest in the farm,
    Which proves his sense ; not like some city fools,
    Who jabber nonsense about crops and cattle,
    Yet know not growing wheat from meadow hay.

Mrs. R. But you monopolize his time too much,
    And trudge him off to see your out-door work,
    When he would rather ride or walk with us.

Rivers. Go on, find fault, do !   Am I ever right ?

Mrs. R. You need not be offended.   I admit
    That in his pleasant face, and graceful manners,
    And style of dress, I see much to commend ;

And if he is received in good society,
I am not sorry we invited him.

Rivers. I, heartily, am glad.   But what says Mary ?

Mrs. R. Nothing, tho' plain enough she deeply feels.
Dear Mrs. Wilder, with her cheerful laugh,
And simple Waters, with his bashful look,
(A little touched with jealousy, I think)
They certainly observe it.

Rivers. Well, and Wilder,
Whom you uphold the tiptop pick of men ?

Mrs. R. Too prudent to obtrude his thoughts unasked.

Rivers. Carryl salutes him with polite reserve,
A finer scorn than open disrespect.

Mrs. R. You are as pertinacious as a fly.
Once get a silly notion in your head,
You never change.   Why nurse this prejudice ?

Rivers. He smiles too often, flatters overmuch.
Give me the man who has degrees of praise,
Who sometimes scowls, or bluntly tells his mind,
As if his heart were in't, and I shall like him :
I hate your smooth-tongued, too obliging fellows,
Your soft-voiced men, afraid to speak aloud.

Mrs. R. Stop, husband, stop, or you will be my death.
                    [*Enter* JAKE.

Jake. Jes' six minits an' haf by dis watch, an' Massa
Jon'than he hoe a' de corn.   Want to know what
he do nex' time, massa.

Rivers. Well, I shall see about it presently.
    10

Mrs. R. Where is Miss Mary?

Jake. Dunno 'xactly, missus.

Rivers. Where Mr. Carryl?

Jake. Guess he a-walkin' whar' young missus be.

Mrs. R. How do you like him, Jake?

Jake. Don' see how a feller gets clear o' likin him.

Mrs. R. How so?

Jake. He talk good to ebry body—gib me a quarter—
                              [*Showing the money.*

He no great man as Massa Wilda.

Rivers. Why not?

Jake. He neber gib nobody nuffin; push we, jes sah
[*imitating the manner*] whan white folks no see.
                              [Mrs. RIVERS *smiles.*

Don' like him, no how you can fix it, shuah.

Rivers. Thus you indulge his unbecoming freedom:
How can your dignity descend so low?

Mrs. R. I wish you would not make ill-natured speeches.

Rivers. Begone.   [*Exit* JAKE.

Mrs. R. Why are you so uncouth and rough?

Rivers. Shall I take lessons from—goodness forbid!

        [*Exit* RIVERS. Mrs. RIVERS *resumes her seat.*
        MARY *and* CARRYL *come up the lawn.*

Carryl. Thy smile is sunshine. See, at thy approach
The flowers of June with fragrance lade the air,
As if in homage to thy gentle tending.

Mary. We had a pleasant walk.

Carryl. Indeed, delightful.

While gazing on the charming scenes around,
The historian's page, the poet's glowing line,
And wild invention of romancer's wit,
Have lost their relish ; and the crowded city
No more attracts me.   Here, my mind aspires
With thoughts more lofty than I dare express.
Auspicious day ! a stranger, and to meet
A welcome so sincere !   Oh ! I shall learn
The farmer's toil—to plough, to hoe, to harrow,
To plant and reap, and gather harvests in ;
But I am ignorant yet.   Will you not teach me ?

Mary. Ah ! there I must refer you to my father.

Carryl. I never wish to see the town again.

Mary. Wilder and you of old were college mates ?

Carryl. In many thoughts we did not sympathize ;
Hence, not close friends.

Mary. You undervalue him.

Carryl. I knew not of his whereabout till now.

Mary. A ruling elder in the Baptist Church,
Teacher in Sunday-school and Bible-classes.
Cling near to him ; he well deserves your favor.

[MRS. RIVERS *comes forward.*

I was commending Wilder to our guest.

Mrs. R. A gentleman by all the country prized ;
Be kind to him, of you he kindly spoke.
He lately married here, his wife a Pawling,
My ancestors and hers were cordial friends
Before the Revolutionary War.

His ample means, joined to her large estate,
Enable them to entertain their guests
In sumptuous style.   We have few men like Wilder.
          [*Enter* RIVERS.

Rivers. Work on the farm—I must be everywhere—
Makes me appear an inattentive host ;
But no neglect to you.   How passed the time ?

Carryl. Awhile I strayed along the Hudson's side,
Then joined Miss Rivers in her morning walk.

Mrs. R. How like you Weeloundell ?

Carryl. A lovely spot.
Often in summer I have passed this place,
Yet scarcely noted from the steamer's deck,
Its wondrous beauty ; never knew till now
(What they who sail the river little know)
The quiet yet active grandeur of the shore ;
By toil improved and excellent taste adorned.

Mrs. R. This property my great-grandfather purchased ;
The original mansion stood down in the valley,
This, built five years ago, is more commodious.

Carryl. And, madam, elegant without pretence.

Mrs. R. Still, we retain the old name—very Scotch—
Perhaps now less expressive.

Carryl. Wee-loun-dell !
How sweet it sounds, and musical withal ;
In fine accord with your attractive home.

Mrs. R. Our present site affords extensive views
And scenes historical within its range.

Rivers. Observe the Lighthouse, built on Stony Point;
    There Wayne surprised and beat the royal troops—
    A deed of danger won with little cost.

Carryl. But noble daring.

Rivers. A rough rock to scale
    On a dark night, with swampy ground in front.
    Look down the river; that is Tappan Zee.
    The *Vulcan* anchored there; yon, Teller's Point,
    Where Andre landed.   Some miles farther south
    Is Tarrytown; the spy was captured there
    By three true lads, whose motive some condemn,
    I swear unjustly.

Carryl. Where met he with Arnold?

Rivers. At Haverstraw,
    Inland a mile—I wish I had my glass.   [*Exit* MARY
    One step this way; observe a dark stone building—
    That is the place; we call it Treason Hill.

Carryl. And this is so?

Rivers. At least so say the people;
    As true, perhaps, as our historians write.
    Another time, and very near the spot,
    A little to the left—you see the house—
        [*Enter* JAKE *with the spyglass.*

Jake. Glass young missus sen', shuah.

       [RIVERS *takes the glass and hands it to* CARRYL.

Carryl. Thank you, sir.

Rivers. Look! Washington once held his quarters there.

Carryl. That name awakes in every heart a thrill;

His life a proud example to the world,
Which all the world reveres.

Rivers. [*To* JAKE.] Why do you laugh?

Jake. Dunno, massa.

Rivers. Be still, you ebon rogue.

Carryl. Nay, chide him not, for rather should we wonder
He did not laugh.   I marvel at myself
That vainly I attempt to praise the man
Above all praise; but memory here reverts
To him who swayed the fortune of our land,
Upheld its flag, and gave a nation birth.
But one returns to change the hackneyed theme.

[*Re-enter* MARY.

Mrs. R. In sooth, good sir, she is a wayward girl,
Who spends the morning 'neath the blazing sun,
Nursing the flowers at cost of her complexion;
While, in the afternoon, she pores o'er books,
Dimming her eyes.   My child, I sometimes fear
You will look wrinkled ere you pass your teens.

Mary. Dear mother, blame me not; if I employ
Daily an hour among my garden beds,
They will repay me with a liberal store
Of flower and perfume.   While I read, they grow.

Carryl. It were a waste extravagant to wear,
Profusely wear, what your good mother prizes.

Mary. Health in the breeze and beauty in the sun,
Why should I fear them?   Look, this elegant rose,
First of the summer, took its delicate hue

And richest fragrance from the sun and shower ;

                     [*She plucks the rose.*

Then wherefore idly waste the day at home,

When loveliness like this thrives out of doors !

Will you accept it, sir ?

                     [*She gives* CARRYL *the rose.*

Carryl. A thousand thanks ;

With your sweet smile more redolent it comes.

I place it here.

                 [*He puts the rose in his button-hole.*

Mary. Alas ! it soon must wither.

Carryl. Though withered, I shall prize it for your sake.

Mrs. R. Come in, my child, and rest : you must be tired.

Excuse us, gentlemen.

                 [*Exeunt* MRS. *and* MARY RIVERS.

Rivers. Both are excused.

And shall I show my crops ?   You are not tired ?

Carryl. Oh, no ; entirely at your service, sir.

Rivers. First let me give an order in the barn.

I shall detain you but a single moment.   [*Exit*

Carryl. Pity that Wilder shares their best esteem ;

And he is pious, charitable too,

With some additions which make up the saint.

Tho' vicious youth may come to godly age,

It is by slow degrees, not at a jump :

Yet, barely possible, blessed with a wife

As full of innocence as playful mirth,

He, in her virtue, is an altered man.

Strange changes, as exceptions, sometimes happen.
May this be one!

[*Re-enter* RIVERS.

Rivers. The day is ours till dinner.   [*Exeunt.*

SCENE II.—*An Orchard.*

Enter WILDER *in a musing mood.*

Wilder. As I surmised, Carryl, lovesick has come,
　　And me regards with a distrustful eye,
　　Which I return with a complacent smile,
　　To hide my pent-up hate.   Revenge leads **man**
　　Through many dangerous paths to crush his **foe**!
　　I will risk reputation, yea, my life,
　　To thwart the hope of this detested Carryl.
　　But how succeed ?   How keep my hand unseen ?
　　Think, busy brain !   Think, think !   By Jove !   I
　　In Mary's artless disposition sleeps   [have it.
　　A spirit fierce, that quickly would resent
　　Insult or slight—the sharpest chord to strike.
　　Invent a lie, to sting her sense of shame,
　　And wound the family pride ; then, in fit time,
　　Allure her on to draw from me the tale,
　　As if reluctant, under oath of silence.
　　A glorious thought ; my bulwark is her truth.
　　　　　　　[*Enter* WATERS.

Waters. Why, Wilder, did you leave us so abruptly ?
Wilder. My wife and you were busy at croquet,

And, not to spoil your game, I wandered forth
To muse an hour in solitary thought.
We all have serious moments—or should have.

Waters. This letter just received.

                          [*Handing* WILDER *a letter.*

Wilder. [*After reading.*] It comes from Fountain.

Waters. And nothing there to flurry you ?

Wilder. Oh, no.

Waters. You seem a little disconcerted.

Wilder. No.

Waters. Do business men rely on his opinion ?

Wilder. Why, what a question ! He is worth a million.

Waters. Wall Street weighs people in its golden scales.

Wilder. Waters, take my advice, go there ; be weighed ;
    You will score higher than among the wits.

Waters. What does he say ?

Wilder. Stocks still on the advance.

Waters. And he a bear ?

Wilder. You know he is, by nature :
    Wisely, perhaps, for I have heard it said,
    Nine times in ten it is the side to win.

Waters. Since, as you say, you speculate no more,
    What need you care tho' markets rise or fall ?

Wilder. Oh ! I am done with stocks, and had a lesson,
    A costly one, yet not enough to hurt me.
    But this advance has proved a blow to Fountain :
    And he, confessing frankly, asks a loan—
    I fain would help him—of ten thousand dollars.

        10.*

I have not so much money at command ;
My note, if you indorse, will bring the needful.
What say you, Waters ?   You make no reply.
Well, he must struggle on without our aid.

Waters. How comes it, if so rich, he wants to borrow ?

Wilder. The richest may, at times, need ready cash.

Waters. You know that I have formed a partnership
With young Montgomery in the China trade ;
Forbidden, by its terms, to indorse again.
Sorry I must refuse.

Wilder. Well, that is prudent.

Waters. Our business will not start till you retire
The notes—I cannot guess the gross amount—
Which I have heretofore indorsed.

Wilder. Right, right.

Waters. The last will soon mature ?

Wilder. Yes, very soon.

Waters. And will be paid ?

Wilder. Of course, as each falls due.
No more of business now—another time.
Tell me, how speeds your suit at Weeloundell ?

Waters. Small favor there ; she is bewitched with Carryl.

Wilder. So fears my wife, yet we have tried our best ;
But no despair, our efforts will not slack.
I told you once, and now repeat, that man,
Tho' buoyed with present hope, shall not succeed ;
And, when dismissed—not distant is the day—
You hold the foremost place.

Waters. What do you mean ?

Wilder. Pray do not ask too much. If you would thrive
   In love, revenge, or hate—in anything—
   Study the politic art of ignorance.
   See nothing not intended you should see ;
   And nothing hear, but sharply look and listen.
   Take my advice ; I promise you success.
   Resume your game, but do not speak of stocks,
   And not one word of Fountain or his letter.
                              [*Exit* WATERS.
   Confound the news !   I stand on ruin's brink,
   By him seduced to gamble in the stocks,
   Loss followed loss, and deeper down I plunged ;
   Yet here he writes, the sun will shine and bring
   A golden harvest if I send the money.
   I have it not, and no assets to raise it,
   While my dear wife without suspicion laughs.
   Let come what may, they cannot touch her farm,
   That is beyond the reach of sharpers' claws.
                                        [*Exit.*

SCENE III.—*A Parlor.*

MRS. RIVERS *at her knitting.*

Mrs. R. Only by looks has he confessed the love
   Which, unaware, she artlessly returns.
   Sad thought ! When married, I may be alone ;
   The wife must follow where the husband leads.

Tho' Cousin Plume writes warmly in his praise,
She has not once alluded to his kin.
My own forebears were famous at the Bar
And in the Senate ; in this county dwelt
Respected, rich, a hundred years ago :
I would not have my china mate with delf,
Tho' richly gilt.   You had a weary walk.

   [*Enter* RIVERS *and* CARRYL.

Carryl. A long, long walk, but not a weary one.
The many charming sights beguiled fatigue.

Mrs. R. I prithee, sit.   [CARRYL *takes a chair.*

Rivers. I showed him everything ;
The wheat, the oats, the rye, the hay, and corn,
The apple orchard and potato field ;
Our cattle, too, which I was proud to show.

Carryl. And my unskilful eye saw, at a glance,
That labor promises a rich return.

   [*Enter* MARY *and* MRS. WILDER *with flowers.*

Mrs. R. Glad to see you.

Mrs. W. And I not sad to come.
  [*To* MR. RIVERS.] How do you do, sir ?

Rivers. Always hale and hearty.

Mrs. W. And pray, my new acquaintance, how are you ?

Carryl. I thank you, madam, well.

Mrs. R. [*Looking at the flowers.*] A pretty show ;
Fragrant and fresh they bloom.

Mrs. W. Yes, thank this child :
She, in our rambles, gathered every one.

[*To Carryl.*] Admire them, sir ; they teach us va-
    rious lessons :
The sunflower, pride ; humility, the broom ;
The lily. purity ; the myrtle, love.
You have seen flowers before—of course you have,
At funerals and weddings.
Mary. How you talk !   [them ?
Mrs. W. Where else have city beaux a chance to see
Mary. At balls and routs rich flowers adorn the rooms,
    And ladies wear the rarest of the season.
Mrs. W. If they are young and have a liberal beau.
Mary. Or generous father.
Mrs. R. You will have your jest.
Mrs. W. Well, I have done, and here I lay them down.
                [*She places them on a table.*
    And she, with some assistance, may arrange
            [*Glancing at* MARY *and then at* CARRYL.
    A fine bouquet to grace the dinner-table.
    [*To* CARRYL.] Ah, sir ! you seem fatigued.
Carryl. I thank you, no ;
    Not very tired.
Rivers. Yes. tired with our long tramp.
Mrs. W. This is indeed a pleasant resting-place.
    May I sit down ? Let jealousy object.
              [*She takes a seat beside him.*
    Husband is absent, and my silly cousin
    Wanders, the Lord knows where, so out I came,
    And meeting Mary, I convoyed her home,

Just for a change and a familiar chat.

Carryl. We had some pleasant times at Mrs. Plume's.

Mary. And met the best society in town.

Mrs. W. And saw extravagance in silks and satins,
With countless vain et cætera besides.

Mary. I scarce imagine how the rich contrive
Such tasteful luxuries and superb adornments.

Mrs. W. Gracious! they never think; do they not pay
Painters, guilders, confectioners, and cooks,
With troops of milliners, to think for them?
Heaven bless the husbands!

Mary. You are too severe.

Mrs. W. No, not a whit; these eyes have seen it all.

Mary. Ladies we often met, refined, well read—

Mrs. W. In volumes vast of—latest Paris fashions.
Oh! very sage while they can dash and flare:
But, when reverses come, then is—dash-down.

Rivers. If they took my advice they would reform.

Mrs. W. Sir, good advice more precious is than gold;
But no one wants it.

Rivers. That I have heard before.

Mrs. W. Find something new, step up above the sun;
The wise man says, nothing is new beneath.

Mrs. R. I hate vulgarities of sudden wealth.

Mrs. W. [*To* CARRYL.] How is my old admirer, Harry
Not married yet?   [Cyprus?

Carryl. A bachelor confirmed.
His tastes still on the toilet and the table.

Mrs. W. The man who jumped into the bramble bush—
　　See nursery rhyme—was not so wondrous wise.
　　Give him a peach or pear, at sight he tells
　　If north or south side of the tree it grew ;
　　If gathered ripe, or half an hour too soon ;
　　And his vast learning comes through eye and ear,
　　Caught in the narrow circle of his walks :
　　For he ne'er read a volume in his life.

Carryl. These harmless foibles only hurt himself.

Mrs. W. But I assure you he was never wrong ;
　　If any pate holds knowledge more than his, [room.
　　Why, he will swear you down, 'tis not worth brain-

Rivers. The man too wise to learn will die a fool.

Mrs. W. We often differed, then I cried, "Bad shoe!"

Mary. Of Cinderella's slipper I have heard,
　　But not of the Bad shoe.

Mrs. W. Old as the hills.
　　Once on a time—thus all true tales begin—
　　A father gave his child, some four years old,
　　A pair of pretty red morocco shoes :
　　She put them on and off a dozen times
　　In infantine delight, till, in her haste,
　　She turned her little foot awry and—pulled.
　　The more she pulled, the less it would go on ;
　　Then, red with rage, she dashed the shoe away,
　　And, in a petty fury, screamed Bad shoe !
　　The father saw a precious lesson here :
　　He took the shoe and put it on with ease,

And asked, " Is it bad daughter or bad shoe ? "
The child, abashed, sobbed out, " Bad daughter,
But Cyprus never would confess so much.   [papa."

Rivers. A first-rate story, excellently told.

Mrs. W. Good listeners, sir, make pleasant company.
But men will talk.

Rivers. Of course—but women, never.

Mrs. W. Very good, sir, very : give me your hand.
He is a dear, kind soul—I mean young Waters.
Miss Mary tells me he was called, in town,
The useful beau ; well, he deserves the title.

Mary. I often blamed the girls, for they were cruel
To laugh, behind his back, for all the pains
He took to please them.

Carryl. A clever man.

Mrs. W. In Yankee sense, a very clever man ;
And many equally—incompetent.

Mary. You love to tease, yet always in good humor,
And say far harsher things than you intend.

Mrs. W. Oh ! worse men—many—could we only find

Rivers. [*Aside.*] Sarcastic still.   [them.

Mrs. W. I tell you, men are moles ;
In others seldom see faults like their own,
Or virtues praise, if innocent of them ;
But vices they confess not, loudly censure.
We are discerning ; at a glance perceive,
Through thin disguise, your fondness, guile, or folly,
And you in blessed ignorance rest the while.

May goodness mend your wits.

Rivers. Mend both.

Mrs. W. Amen !

I have told Waters this a thousand times.

Rivers. And not offended ?

Mrs. W. No : poor, silly soul !

He did not even laugh. I speak in sport,

And never tease him—more than I can help.

Mrs. R. It seems to me mirth is your only tune.

Mrs. W. And sweeter music than a doleful dirge.

I cannot see how women mope at home,

Fretted with trifles and domestic cares :

The gardener lazy, or the footman sour,

The housemaid saucy, or the dinner spoiled.

I make the best of it, and hope to-morrow

Will mend their manners.

Mrs. R. If you, like me,

Were plagued by wasteful, rude, and stupid servants,

You would lose patience too.

Mrs. W. Pray be content ;

For what we cannot cure, they say, endure.

I shall not turn reformer ; if I did,

Mistress and maid alike should share the blame ;

But useless altercations I detest.

O bless my stars ! 'tis near our dinner hour ;

Good-by, dear Mary ; I must hurry home.   [sir,

To all adieu. [*To* CARRYL.] You shall be welcome,

But not alone : be sure—I give you warning—

Come when you may, bring me *a fair* excuse.

Again, good-by to all.   [*Exit* MRS. WILDER.

Mary. A merry heart.

Mrs. R. At times, perhaps, a little too severe.

Carryl. Yet pertinent.

Rivers. Often impertinent.

> [MARY *and* CARRYL *retire to the table.* MARY
> *makes a bouquet of the flowers.*

Mrs. R. Why do you use a phrase so impolite?

Rivers. Whatever word I use, of course 'tis wrong.

If from a ploughman or a hind I differ,

In your opinion each is right, not I.

If sometimes I rebuke obtrusive fools,

You tartly blame me, nor a moment dream

From what deserved censure I refrain ;

But, like a proud, cross wife, still finding fault.

Mrs. R. We are too many here.

> [*Exeunt* MR. *and* MRS. RIVERS.

Mary. What, are they gone?

Carryl. This is indeed with taste and skill arranged.

Mary. You like it? really a sweet bouquet.

Do you delight in flowers?

Carryl. When you are near.

Mary. Not for themselves?

Ah! you prefer to ponder over books.

Carryl. Believe me, I am not an earnest student;

But in my library I love to stray

As in a garden, and, from various shelves,

10

I gather flowers of eloquence and song,
  To please my fancy and improve my mind.
Mary. But you must learn to love these precious gems,
  To court the sunshine and refreshing breeze,
  To seek out-doors the happiness and health
  That rarely visit the dull scholar's cell.
  Which of our poets do you most admire ?
Carryl. Leave them to fame, for only in your smile
  Am I inspired.
Mary. Have you no favorite ?
Carryl. Among the gifted, it is hard to choose.
Mary. See, [*Taking up a book*] this is Bryant's poems
    richly bound ;
  He dearly loves the flowers ; read me some lines.
Carryl. You are my book, and in your face I read
  All that delights and sanctifies the soul.
Mary. O wild enthusiast ! this is mere romance :
  Deny me not.
Carryl. When next we meet in town.
Mary. Indeed, you have not overstayed your welcome,
  Nor have you visited the scenes renowned
  Father intends to show ; nor have you heard
  The famous Revolutionary tales
  (For this, you know, is called the Neutral Ground)
  Some never penned, the people here relate.
Carryl. He is too kind.   [*A bell sounds.*
Mary. The preparation bell :
  You have just half an hour to dress for dinner.
                                            [*Exit.*

Carryl. What native grace and dignity of mien!
　'Tis not her seraph-voice, nor lovely smile,
　No, nor the fascination of her eye,
　That thrills my heart with rapture undefined.
　But hope, beyond the curb of reason, flies
　Like fleecy clouds, chased by the furious wind,
　Along the pathless azure, toward a goal
　They never reach—but into air dissolve.　[*Exit.*

SCENE IV.—*A Library.*

Enter WILDER, *agitated.*

Wilder. Shall I without an effort sink to ruin?
　By the cold world be laughed at for a fool?
　Or be like borrower or beggar spurned?
　Thank my bright stars! I have too proud a spirit.
　So closely I can imitate his hand,
　The subtlest clerk would swear that Waters wrote it.
　It must be done; how else escape disgrace?
　If not the safest, 'tis my only course.
　　　　　　[*Sits at the table to write.*
　If paid when due, what wrong have I committed?
　Detection is the crime.　It has been done
　A thousand times before: what noise is that?
　　　　　　[*Rises in alarm, and looks around.*
　I am a coward: not a soul is near.
　　　　　　[*Resumes his seat, and writes.*
　This is my note, and that is his indorsement.
　　　　　[*Rings; writes a letter and incloses the note.*

If the worst come, I shall make Waters swear
That he indorsed it.   Hurry for the mail.
[*Enter a servant, who receives the letter, then exit.*
Free of a mountain load, I bound again,
Light as a fairy on a moonlit hill.
The foul fiend I defy.
   [*Enter another servant.* WILDER *starts.*
       Curse my weak nerves.
Servant. Farmer Greenlake is below.
Wilder. Show him up.   [*Exit servant.*
Why does that boor intrude ?   He troubles me ;
Yet I must treat him civilly, at least.
    [*Enter* GREENLAKE.
Neighbor Greenlake, glad to see you.   What news ?
Greenl. The farm is sold.
Wilder. And how much did it bring ?
Greenl. Five hundred dollars—just the price you named.
Wilder. How land advances !   You paid only forty.
Greenl. That was ten years ago.
Wilder. How many acres ?
Greenl. Twenty.
Wilder. You must be rich.   All paid in cash ?
Greenl. Is that check good ? [*Showing a check.*
Wilder. Yes ; for ten thousand dollars,
 And certified besides ; good as the bank.
 I know the drawer—a peculiar man.
Greenl. He offered that—out came his watch—and said,
 I give you forty seconds to decide ;

Accept, refuse ; I care not which you do.
No time to waste ; I never chaffer long.
His very words.

Wilder. Never an hour to spare,
For so he says.   Need you the money, neighbor ?

Greenl. The interest only.

Wilder. Then take my advice.

Greenl. Just what I came to ask, for you know best.

Wilder. Lend it on bond and mortgage ; that is safe.
But let me see ; the tax on mortgage loans—
An unjust law—eats half the interest up.

Greenl. Find me a good investment.

Wilder. Let me think :
One I can trust—in town ; a banker, rich ;
Perhaps he might oblige.

Greenl. Talk not of him ;
Your note is all I want.

Wilder. Neighbor, sit down.   [*Rings.*
I have not seen your face for many a day.

Greenl. Spring work, you know, keeps farmers busy, sir.

Wilder. Why, spring is past ; this is the month of June.
How look the crops ?

Greenl. I can not well complain.

Wilder. You are a thriving man.   [*Enter a servant.*
A cup of coffee.

Greenl. Thank you, no ; not for me.

Wilder. No trouble, sir.   [*Exit servant.*
Bourbon you may prefer.

Greenl. I never drink.

Wilder. Therefore you are a happy, prosperous man.

　　　[Re-enter servant with coffee, and retires.

　　The best of Java ; please, sir, try this cup.

　　　　[Fills a cup, and presents it to GREENLAKE.

Greenl. *[Tasting it.]* Oh ! very nice, indeed.

Wilder. More sugar, sir ?

Greenl. Exactly right.　Suppose you give that note.

Wilder. If you insist ; but only to oblige you.

Greenl. With interest, in my favor, on demand.

Wilder. Of course, of course.

　　　[He sits and writes, then, rising, gives GREEN-
　　　　LAKE *the note.*

　　　　　　　　　I think this will suffice.

Greenl. I ask no better ; just as good as gold.

Wilder. Indorse—there is a pen—upon the back.

　　　*[*GREENLAKE *indorses, and hands* WILDER *the
　　　　check.*

　　The cash is always ready when you call ;

　　But, for convenience, give me three days' notice.

Greenl. I may not want the money in a year.

　　Good day, good day.　　　　　　　　　　*[Exit.*

Wilder. Be not a stranger, sir.

　　By Jove, a godsend ! just the sum he needs.

　　Who says I gave not Greenlake good advice ?

　　But, will or nill, he thrust on me the money.

　　Should I fail to repay, misfortune merely,

　　And not in law a crime.

> *[Looks at his watch, and rings.*

'Tis not too late :
This yet may reach the mail.

> *[Enter a servant.*

Harness the horses.

> *[Exit servant.* WILDER *writes a letter.*

That note is mailed—the law forbids recall ;
No matter, I have charged him not to use it.
Now hasten bitter hate to sweet revenge !
Suppose love rages stronger than her truth ; [mine;
There danger lurks. What then ? Her word 'gainst
And mine, like hers, stands here in some repute.
But, once entrapped, she keeps her oath, or dies.
The worst I do defy.

> *[Enter servant.*

Servant. The coach is ready.   *[Exit.*

Wilder. And I am ready too, a fearless man,
Resolved betimes to execute my plan.   *[Exit.*

ACT III.

SCENE I.—*The Music Room.*

MARY *seated at the piano.*

After striking a few chords, she rises.

Mary. I cannot sing, my voice is not in tune ;
    For he is absent who inspires my song,
    And thought is weary waiting his return.
    I think he loves me—certain, I love him :
    When in the arbor yestereve we sat,
    I saw confession trembling on his lip ;
    Afraid to hear, what most I wished to hear,
    I turned aside, with palpitating heart,
    And foiled him in his purpose.   Well-a-day !
    Blessed be the hour he came to Weeloundell.
    The bluebird trills more fondly to his mate,
    The south wind softer woos the fluttering leaves,
    The very lawn puts on a fresher green.
    O happy me ! a new existence dawns !
          [*Enter* WILDER.   [enter ;

Wilder. Though unannounced, yet, neighbor-like, I
    But pardon me ; have I disturbed your music ?

11

Mary. No, no, indeed.

Wilder. I find you once alone.

Mary. Mother is busy with the house affairs,
        And father with his guest is in the fields ;
        Please take a seat, for they will soon return.
        What ails you, sir ? Why you seem quite down-
        Your wife, I hope, is well.   [hearted:

Wilder. I thank you, well.
        I left her at a game of chess with Waters.

Mary. Unpleasant news from town ?

Wilder. Oh, no, Miss Mary.

Mary. Did I not prize you as a neighbor, proved
        For gentle feeling and a heart sincere,
        I should not question thus ; but by your looks
        I fear some trouble labors in your mind
        And mars its peace.

Wilder. Sorry that I intrude,
        Since your observant eye has marked my looks.

Mary. Rely on mother's sympathy and mine.
        Dear me ! a serious ill ?

Wilder. Pray do not ask.
        Seek not to draw from me my painful thoughts,
        Which I would fain conceal : for if I spoke,
        It might afflict your trusting heart to learn
        That, where we most confide, yea, where we love,
        We are deceived.

Mary. You never were deceived,
        Why you have not an enemy on earth.

Wilder. The best may be maligned.

Mary. Are you maligned ?

Wilder. If 'twere no more, I should not waste a thought,
Save to devise a means to melt his hate,
And his good will regain.

Mary. A golden rule.

Wilder. When calumny assails,
From an unlooked-for source, a sinless maid
(Constrained in silence to lament the wrong
Which we have not the privilege to redress)
The true man will, in sympathy, be sad.

Mary. No man so base—the world is much abused ;
The little birds that warble on their perch,
Or wing through air, are innocent as gay ;
The flowers of spring turn smiling to the sun,
And welcome honey-bees to sip their sweets ;
No discord jars in nature's marvellous choir.

Wilder. Some fruits we prize, delicious to the taste,
And several flowers, delightful to the eye,
Yield, to the chemist's art, a fatal poison.

Mary. Oh, not a word of that will I believe.

Wilder. You lead a tranquil, unsuspicious life,
Among dear friends, and all—excepting one—
Like you, have no disguise.

Mary. Excepting one ?

Wilder. I pray you, pardon me :
Live long in unbelief, still think the world
Pure, as it seems in your ideal dream.

I did not mean to hint my cause of sadness,
Nor cloud your sunny days with slanderous tales.
But, change the subject ; my respect for you
Forbids me to discuss unpleasant themes.

Mary. I do not understand : more I must learn.

Wilder. Forget what I have said ; I am too hasty.

Mary. A mystery here I fail to comprehend.

Wilder. Pity, my looks awaken your suspicion,
And pity I have breathed a thought aloud.

Mary. You long have been a counsellor, a guide,
And, with a brother's tenderness, reproved
Through happy years my girlish pranks and whims ;
If I am worthy, if you are unchanged,
Speak plainly out, and free me from suspense.

Wilder. Would that the art were mine to hide my feelings !
Then your close questions had not trapped my
To hint my sorrow.   [tongue

Mary. This is more than strange !
Are you my friend ?

Wilder. Why ask ? You know I am.

Mary. Then prove it, sir.

Wilder. Patience, I implore.

Mary. From other lips this had not cost a pang ;
But, from a man so just, I greatly fear
There is a grievance hid.

Wilder. Do not insist.

Mary. If you have heard a whisper 'gainst my truth,
A breath to raise a blush on virtue's cheek,

A word which casts a shadow on our house,
Declare it instantly.

Wilder. Be not so eager ;
You are too strongly moved : dear Mary, wait.

Mary. Give me your thought. I will not wait a
moment.

Wilder. In this fierce mood—I never saw before—
If told, I fear you might unwisely act.

Mary. Trust in my prudence, my discretion trust.

Wilder. Some other time—not now—perhaps, to-morrow.

Mary. Speak now. You shall ! I will not be denied.

Wilder. You press on me a most ungracious task,
And I perforce must yield, if—you will promise—

Mary. Promise ! Sir, I will swear.

Wilder. If you will swear
By word or act you never will divulge,
Nor by vague sign give the remotest hint,
For man or woman to divine the secret
Which you so earnestly demand from me ;
But, in good faith, will follow my advice—

Mary. Go on—go on ! My hands are raised to heaven.

Wilder. Thus as you stand before His sacred throne,
Here I accept your inarticulate oath.
Art sworn ?   [*A Tableau.*

Mary. Amen ! I am.

Wilder. Now listen calmly.
There is one here on business with your father—

Mary. Do you refer to Edward Carryl, sir ?

Wilder. Judge for yourself.   In an unhallowed place,
    Among the vile—viler than I dare breathe
    To modest ear, he made your name a jest,
    ('Twas in the city, during springtime past)
    And vainly boasted that a country girl
    Annoyed him with her love ; who, at his beck,
    Would leap into his arms.   Nightly, as he
    From your pure presence sought that den of vice,
    He was saluted by a painted troop,
    " How is the country girl ?"   " Oh ! lovesick still,"
    He laughing cried, and all in chorus joined.

Mary. Where shall I go—where hide my head from
    shame ?

Wilder. Among the beaux you met at Mrs. Plume's.
    Some were his fit associates, though they seemed
    To blush embarrassed when a lady speaks ;
    They heard the slander, and, unmanly, mean,
    When they observed you smile—as oft you did—
    On the traducer—

Mary. Oh !

Wilder. Exchanged sly glances—

Mary. Spare me, oh ! spare me this.

Wilder. And he, besides,
    Spoke of your family with disrespect :
    Purse proud, he said, vain of patrician blood,
    When—were the truth confessed—first of their race,
    An exile came from Scotland, friendless, poor :
    But skill in peddling saved him from starvation ;

Till, by a dash—in trade—he missed a prison,
And, from his—profits—bought a tract of land
With humble cottage—hence named Weeloundell.
A spacious mansion lately has been built,
To gratify a proud, ambitious dame,
Where now they live in style ; the advance in land
Has made them wealthy, and their upstart pride
Aspires to rank with ancients of the soil.

Mary. No, no ; impossible ! It is not true.
   My heart will break ! He could not be unjust.

Wilder. I wonder not you disbelieve and weep ;
It grieved my soul to see that very man
Crawl, serpent-like, beneath the sacred roof
To sting you deeper, that my tell-tale face
Betrayed the indignation swelling here :
And, scarce aware, you wrung from me reluctant
The foul-mouthed slander I should not have told.
Yet, if I had withheld from you the libel,
Would I have been the true friend I profess ?

Mary. How shall I look my mother in the face ?

Wilder. Do nothing rashly ; you have freely sworn.

Mary. Distracted, lost, I know not what I did.

Wilder. My short experience teaches me a maxim,
That, to redress or contradict a lie,
Is nearest kin to an outrageous slander.
Thousands who never heard the original tale
Might hearken our defence, and thus it spreads.
Man is a scandal lover ; some enjoy,

As a delicious dish, a false report.
And, with a show of lip-deep sympathy,
Feast on the pangs which they pretend to feel.

Mary. My heart is full—too full.

Wilder. Take my advice :
Treat him with cold disdain, discard him hence,
And, for a swift revenge, marry—marry—
When you shall meet one worthy of your love :
Your beauty may command. Breathe not aloud,
Nor mutter in your dreams what I have told.
I am amazed ! Where is your woman pride ?
'Twill be a nine days' wonder and forgotten ;
The world will right you in becoming time.
Be like yourself.

　　　　　　[JAKE *has been listening, unseen.*

Jake. Young missus no sick—shuah.   [*Exit.*

Mary. This bitter insult mother will resent,
But crushed and humbled, I can only weep.

　　　　　　　　[MARY *rushes out.*

Wilder. She feels the sting : it works to admiration !
But caution whispers, quickly steal away ;
None should suspect I have been here to-day.
Ah ! I am caught—How is my old acquaintance ?

　　　　　　　[*As he is going, enter* CARRYL.

Carryl. Sir, I am well.

Wilder. A bright and pleasant morning.
Commissioned by my wife, I seek Miss Rivers,
A fair and comely maid, a peerless damsel.

Carryl. The summer's sun shines not upon a fairer.

Wilder. You may indeed say so.   Fortunate man—
  , She smiles on you, I saw that at a glance.

Carryl. I dare not aim so high.

Wilder. Sir ! you are modest.

  It is a common phrase, and true withal,
  The coyish maiden, though by twenty loved,
  In time weds one ; the rest may hang or drown.
  I give you joy.

Carryl. For what ?

Wilder. Old college chums,

  We should not meet as strangers : be assured,
  You have already won the old folks' favor,
  And that is half the battle.

Carryl. Whither drive you ?

Wilder. No matter now, our honored hostess comes.

  Madam, you see, unushered I have entered.

          [*Enter* MRS. RIVERS.

Mrs. R. You never do intrude ; how is your wife ?

Wilder. I thank you, well ; I call, by her request,

  To ask Miss Rivers' company this morning :
  Our yacht is stanch and strong—a lovely day,
  With a fresh, favoring breeze.

Mrs. R. I will inquire.   [*Rings the bell.*

  No doubt she will accept.

Wilder. [*Aside.*] A shrewd excuse.

      [*To* MRS. R.] Madam, I promise her a pleasant sail.
          11*

*[Enter a Maid-servant. Mrs. Rivers speaks
        to her. Exit Maid.*

Wilder. [*To* Carryl.] You will join us; we have a
    seat reserved.

Carryl. My host and hostess may dispose of me.

Wilder. How is your excellent husband ?

Mrs. R. Always well,
    And, farmer-like, is busy in the fields.

Carryl. His taste and skill and his unwearied toil
    Are everywhere displayed, and Weeloundell
    Blooms like a garden rather than a farm.

        [Re-enter Maid hurriedly.

Maid. O ma'am ! O ma'am !

Mrs. R. Be more respectful, girl.

Maid. Miss Mary sure is sick : she sits alone
    In deep distress, and bitterly she weeps.

Mrs. R. What is the matter ? Did she not explain ?

Maid. She nothing said, nor even looked at me,
    But wept and sobbed as if her heart would break.

Wilder. A momentary ill ; I trust, no more.

Mrs. R. She must be sick : excuse me, gentlemen.
    No time for ceremony.

            [Exeunt Mrs. Rivers *and Maid.*

Wilder. A sudden ailment.

Carryl. An hour ago I saw her well and happy ;
    Very sudden.

Wilder. I hope not serious,
    But I must hasten to inform my wife ;

She will be sorry Mary is not well.

We shall be glad to see you.

Carryl. Sir, good morning.   [*Exit.*

Wilder. That gush of feeling, rife in love-sick girls,

    Will soon subside, too violent to last.

    Amused with new conceits and pleasant themes,

    The heart forgets ; extremes beget extremes.

                                     [*Exit.*

SCENE II.—*An Antechamber.*

MARY seated in deep distress.

Mary. What have I heard ?   Bound by an oath pro-

    fane.   [head ?

    O'erwhelmed with shame, where shall I hide my

    Where find a balm for wretchedness like mine ?

    Oh, I have lived too long !   Why was it told ?

    No, no, not true—he could not be so cruel,

    His sweet looks, else, are falser than his tongue.

    Could I confide this secret to my mother,

    Her kind compassion might assuage my grief ;

    But 'tis forbid—in silence I must suffer.

    Why did I swear ?   I sooner would accuse

    Wilder of fraud than Carryl charge with slander.

    If guilty ! down, oh traitress thought away,

    My heart would not believe though he confessed.

    But I am to discard him : shall we part !

    One only choice—despair but not dishonor—

And, struggling with my bitter tears, I wait
Till heaven vouchsafes forgetfulness and rest.

[She sinks upon the sofa.

[Enter MRS. RIVERS *and Maid.*

Mrs. R. What is the matter, Mary? tell me, child.
Why do you wring your hands? Why this distress?
Turn not your face away, but look on me—
You gaze bewildered through a flood of tears,
As if some frightful accident or ill
Had suddenly befallen. Art sick or hurt?

Mary. I am not sick, yet know not what I am.   [me;

Mrs. R. Why these convulsive sobs? Hide nothing from
Who should a daughter trust, if not her mother?

Mary. In time, if that time comes, you shall learn all.

Mrs. R. It is unkind to keep me in suspense.

Mary. Forgive me, mother; oh, forgive my silence.

Maid. Dear me, how can I help?

Mrs. R. Unlace her dress;
She will the freer breathe.

Mary. No, no; no use.

Mrs. R. I cannot see you suffer.

Mary. Leave me, leave me.

Maid. What shall I do?

Mrs. R. Fetch me some water, quick. *[Exit Maid.*
You will feel better when I bathe your head.

Mary. I feel no pain—not in the head—not there.

Mrs. R. Your mind seems wandering in a feverish
dream.

Mary. And when I waken, mother, I shall win,
    At least deserve your pity, not reproof.
Mrs. R. More and still more perplexed.

        [Re-enter Maid with a basin of water.
        MRS. RIVERS *offers to bathe her head.*

Mary. Take it away.
Mrs. R. Do not refuse—it will refresh your spirits.
Mary. Pray, let me weep alone.
Mrs. R. Send for the doctor.   *[To the Maid.*
Mary. Stay, stay: no medicine will reach my wound—
    It lies too deep.
Mrs. R. Run for her father: haste.   *[Exit Maid.*
    Never before have you withheld a thought:
    Think of a mother's fears. A secret here!
Mary. Oh! if you knew the misery I endure,
    The pangs that rend my heart, you would forbear.
Mrs. R. Has any one been here to hurt your feelings?
    Has Carryl said a word, or looked unkind?
Mary. To me—never.
Mrs. R. He is a charming man.
Mary. I will not sail in Mrs. Wilder's yacht.
Mrs. R. Well, well, if not to-day, perhaps to-morrow,
    When you are better.
Mary. Is her husband gone?
Mrs. R. Has he been rude? Oh, no, impossible!
    We always look to him for good advice.
Mary. If gone—send for him, not a moment lose.

[*Enter* RIVERS.

Rivers. Wife, is she very ill?

Mrs. R. Be not alarmed:
  A sudden fit, hysterical, I think,
  And not uncommon at her time of life.

Rivers. Sprinkle her face with ice-cold water—hurry,
  An excellent remedy.

Mrs. R. Do not disturb her;
  For she persistently rejects my aid.

Rivers. An hour ago you were as blithe and gay
  As bees among the flowers; why now in tears?

Mrs. R. Something has happened to distress her mind.

Rivers. What! a lover's quarrel! [*To* MARY.] Have you
      been slighted?
  Come, tell me, daughter, who has been uncivil?

Mary. Ask not: till Wilder comes my lips are sealed.

Mrs. R. On his good judgment she relies.

Rivers. On his!

Mrs. R. And wishes to consult with him.

Rivers. With him!
  We are as competent to give advice
  As that much-landed man.' Confide in us.

Mary. Send, I insist: say I demand his presence.

Rivers. I never heard her so imperative.

Mrs. R. Wait till to-morrow.

Mary. No: to-day—this hour!

Rivers. Wife, you are right, it is hysteria.

Mrs. R. Do not refuse—pray gratify her wish.

Rivers. All I possess on earth is yours, dear child,
    And all would give to see you well and happy;
    If Wilder can allay this nervous feeling,
    Though 'gainst my judgment, I will send for him.
                        [*Exit* RIVERS.

Mary. Go leave me, mother, to my gloomy thoughts.

Mrs. R. I cannot leave you, child: come to your cham-
    And rest awhile: the moment Wilder comes   [ber
    I promise you shall see him.

Mary. Here will I wait.   [ment,

Mrs. R. Though, as your father said, against my judg-
    I will not thwart you in this frame of mind.
                      [*Exit* MRS. RIVERS.

Mary. One must be innocent! I am unjust
    To linger here supine, in fruitless tears:
    What base and sinful motive prompted him
    To bind me by an oath? He shall absolve me!
    Justice divine! aid my determined purpose
    To unmask the false and vindicate the true.
    He must return; till then, where shall I wander?
    There is no rest for me, here—anywhere. [*Exit.*

SCENE III.—*The Highway leading to Railroad Depot.*
        Enter WILDER.

Wilder. Waters must watch her mood, declare himself,
    And slighted love, in spite, accepts; when married,
    The lies I uttered, like forgotten tales,
    Will never, ghost-like, rise to witness 'gainst me.

Though here triumphant, should I fail elsewhere,
How cover my disgrace ?   There is one way—
But I must live to reimburse young Waters ;
His loss by me her portion will repay,
And more, he wins the idol of his heart.
Bad as I am, relentless though my hate,
I am not guilty of ingratitude.
Ah ! worthy cousin.

                 [*Enter* WATERS.

Waters. How ! You seem disturbed.

Wilder. I am : this moment come from Weeloundell,
And left Miss Mary in extreme distress ;
Wherefore, I do not clearly understand :
But this surmise, she has discarded Carryl,
Or soon will do it.   Hasten thither—go !
She needs a tenant for a vacant heart.

Waters. Carryl dismissed ?   For what slight or offence ?

Wilder. Inquire of them : I am not in their secrets.
If they desire to see me, make the excuse
That I have visitors and cannot leave them.

Waters. Shall I say this ?

Wilder. No questions ask, but go !
A civil plea ; and means, I will not come.
You will learn more than I have time to tell.

                    [*Exit* WATERS.

Prudence cries, Stay.—keep from her sight awhile.
Waters will soon return : from his report
I may infer how my invention thrives.

But other thoughts perplex and haunt my mind—
Gamble in stocks! trust him as an expert!
More safely might we bet on sharper's card,
Then are we sure what on each stake we lose;
But, in the stocks, we play 'gainst loaded dice,
And know not what we risk. Where were my wits?

　　' [*Enter* FOUNTAIN, *with a valise.*

Dropped from the clouds, upstarted from the ground.
Whence and when came you?

Foun. By the train from town.　　　　　　[speak?

Wilder. Your presence bodes no good. You heard me

Foun. Mutterings I heard, not an articulate sound;
　　But saw, as I approached—

Wilder. What did you see?

Foun. Some gestures wild, as with yourself you held
　　An argument which seemed to move you deeply.

Wilder. Who could guess better than yourself the cause?
　　You have enticed me onward, step by step,
　　In cursed speculations, till I am
　　Bankrupt in purse, distracted too in mind.
　　What bad news came to tell? Give me the worst:
　　I am prepared for ruin.

Foun. Ruin? pshaw!

Wilder. We are not quite undone? You do not answer;
　　There is a doubt.

Foun. I only came to say
　　What 'twas not well to write—we need more cash.

Wilder. Good heaven! more cash! and ask you more
      from me?
    Had I the ore hid in the Rocky Mountains,
    Ungathered gold in Californian mines,
    The wealth gulped down by the voracious sea,
    It were too poor to meet your vast demands.
    I have no more.   All I remitted lost?
    Greenlake's ten thousand dollars also gone?
    You have not used the note I sent you last,
    Indorsed by Waters?

Foun. Yes, it is discounted.   [you.

Wilder. I charged you not to use it—strictly charged

Foun. In our necessity what could I do?

Wilder. Protect that note.

Foun. Waters has ample means,
    Ten thousand more or less he will not miss;
    His father left him more than he can spend.

Wilder. Can you be secret?   He refused his name,
    And I, with inadvertent haste—

Foun. Well, what?

Wilder. I—I—

Foun. I did not dream of such a thing;
    But blame not me: for your sake I am **sorry**.

Wilder. It must be paid—at any sacrifice.

Foun. Well, show me how.

Wilder. Have you no friends but me?

Foun. Many; but, like ourselves, all short of cash.
    You have no business tact: you little dream

How skilful men manipulate the market ;
What lies invent, what rumors spread abroad,
To scare the timid or appal the bold.

Wilder. I thank my stars ! sad day, the day we met.

Foun. Rail not : good men and bad in every trade,
Lawyer or merchant, minister or thief,
And some as truly pious as yourself.
But I will save you—if I can.

Wilder. How, how ?

Foun. Some men are fertile in expedients,
Who lack the arms to conquer a success.

Wilder. What are the weapons ?

Foun. Cash—the two-edged sword　　　　　　[blocks.
Which cleaves through Wall street's adamantine
Joined with some heavy backers in a ring,
And deftly planned—beyond reach of mischance.
Our part to raise is forty thousand dollars.
It matters not to enter on details
You could not comprehend ; have faith in me.

Wilder. On what security ?

Foun. A mortgage on the farm.

Wilder. Mortgage the ancient homestead of my wife !
I never will : a villain, sir, to ask.

Foun. Talk not so loud ; you will expose yourself.

Wilder. You are in danger if you ask again.

Foun. You need not fume, nor use uncivil threats,
But hear me, or—resign to fate.

Wilder. Go on !

Foun. To be secure from loss by fire, her deeds
      You placed in my proof-safe, and Lawyer Sparks
      From them has drawn the mortgage.   There it is ;
      Examined by the lender and approved.
                         [*Taking the papers from valise.*
Wilder. Merciless knave ! would'st also rob my wife ?
Foun. Before you dashed in this expensive style,
      You should have counted cost ; or, when you found
      The out-go largely overran the income,
      Retrenchment was a virtue ; but false pride,
      To keep appearance up—that was your phrase—
      Daily encroached upon your capital.
      In this dilemma you sought my advice—
      Which I sincerely gave ; but oft good things
      That promise finely disappoint the hope.
      Yet, no despair ; you may command success ;
      Ruin, or forty thousand dollars—choose.
Wilder. Fearful to stand upon the giddy verge
      Of this vast precipice.   Hell yawns beneath.
Foun. She'll sign whate'er you ask without a question ;
      She hates, as oft she says, to think of business.
Wilder. Should she know it !
Foun. Know it, in heaven's name ! how ?
      In sixty days that false note is retired,
      The mortgage cancelled, and your fortune made.
Wilder. Speak not to mortal ; let no living creature
      Suspect I ever ventured in the stocks.
Foun. You rave as if stock-jobbing were a crime.

We break no law—[*Aside.*] though many fools we
Wilder. For mercy, hush !   [break.

[*Enter* MRS. WILDER.

Mrs. W. Gracious ! You in the country ?
  Wall street will fail, or the great city sink ;
  But I am glad to see you.   Waters came
  Last week to waste a month ; stay you as long,
  We shall together have a jovial time.

Foun. No, not so long ; I only came to catch
  One breath of mountain air ; to-night return.

Mrs. W. Run, run ! the city is in danger, run !
  Stay not an hour.   Bless me, I am afraid.
  What will become of all the stay-at-homes ?

Foun. It does me good to hear your cheerful laugh.

Mrs. W. Have your own way, take the first train to town,
  A panic else may turn the street stark mad.

Foun. No danger, madam.

Mrs. W. Oh, sir, you are safe,
  For cousin says you are a millionaire.

Foun. That is easily said.

Mrs. W. Very easily ;
  But Waters is a man of verity,
  Some are more credulous—if we could find them.

Foun. Always, dear madam, in a bantering mood.

Mrs. W. The motive of my life is mirth, not money :
  They tell me, thousands every day are made,
  Or lost, by Wall-street men ; but you are rich,
  One of the thriving ; we poor country folk

Know nothing of the art ; and, for myself,
I nothing wish to know.   The cares of business
Turn people pale and stupid : we are rich,
We are, my dear—in comfort and content.

Wilder. Indeed we are, good wife.

Mrs. W. Sometimes no rain,
Sometimes too much, then honest farmers fret ;
Still grow the crops, still sleep we sound o' nights,
And harvest comes, despite the city's buzz,
That wondrous hive ; more stings than honey there,
If half the truth were told.

Foun. You country ladies
Must miss the social joys of city life.

Mrs. W. O bless you ! no ; I have seen quite enough,
And found they cost, in jealousy and hate,
Much more than they are worth. Stay here awhile,
Our lovely scenery and delightful drives
Will teach you to contemn the hollow pomp
And heartless follies which amuse the town.

Foun. Fashion craves more than our necessities,
And pride in loftiest flight ne'er reached content.

Mrs. W. A broker preaching ! Mercy me ! what next ?
I should not wonder if, ere doomsday comes,
The world became outrageously devout.
I would not give my farm, and its dear quiet,
For all the din and glitter of the town.

Wilder. [*Aside to* FOUNTAIN.] Do you hear that, and
      still ask for the mortgage ?

Mrs. W. What is the matter, dear ?   Upon my word,
    You look as dismal as Black Friday, love.

Wilder. A sudden headache, wife.

                    [*Enter* JAKE.

Mrs. W. Jake, what o'clock is it ?

Jake. [*Pulling out his watch.*] 'Xactly twelve, missus.

Mrs. W. Your watch must go on wheels.

Jake. Guess no, missus—shuah.

Mrs. W. How does it go ?   [say ?

Jake. Like de gem'mans, tick, tick.   What yourn watch

Mrs. W. It swears the sun keeps time.

Jake. Dunno dat, missus ;
    But, shuah, he gib light to ebery day.
    An' de pretty moon watch when he go sleep.

Wilder. How is Miss Rivers ?

Jake. She mouch betta', massa.

Mrs. W. She indisposed !   Why told me not before ?

Wilder. My terrible headache, and our friend's arrival,
    Quite drove it from my mind.
    [*To* JAKE.] What do you want ?

Jake. Young missus want Massa Wilda' come, shuah.

Wilder. Me !   When ?

Jake. Yees ; massa tell, come right away.

Mrs. W. Go, with my compliments ; say, I am sorry
    He is too ill ; I beg they will excuse him.
    If well, he certainly will call to-morrow.

Wilder. [*Aside to* JAKE.] Off ; you are answered.
                [*Exit* JAKE, *with a comical look at* WILDER.
                    Impudent fellow !

Mrs. W. What think you Mary wants ?

Wilder. I do not know.

    Let us go home : this headache is distressing.

Mrs. W. Shall I assist you, dear ?   Lean on my arm.

    There, gently, gently ; do not walk too fast.

    Come, Fountain, come.

                  [*Exeunt* MR. *and* MRS. WILDER.

Foun. I need not follow them.

    I know him like a book ; he will return

    With headache cured, and I shall have the mortgage.

    I have adroitly played the winning card,

    And found, with all his guile, an easy victim.

    My tool, the lender, at the depot waits

    (A cunning plan, by which he profits largely)

    And when she signs, I lodge the deed for record ;

    The cash that hour is mine, and off I fly

    To some retreat beyond the reach of law.

    When Wall street hears that I have failed and fled,

    There will be growls among the wounded bears.

             [*Re-enter* WILDER.

Wilder. One fate pursues me since the day we met :

    Touch what I may, it turns to dust and ashes.

    You are my evil star ; beneath its blaze

    I'm stricken with despair.

Foun. Why, I have seen

    A stormier day, but never man so mad.

Wilder. I feel my fingers tingling, sir, to tear,

    To tear your false heart out ; but I am thought

A man of some repute, respected here
For heaven knows what, yet more than I deserve.
I would, by the infernal, strangle you.
Beware ! tempt me no more.

Foun. You need not threaten,
 Nor in this foolish manner drive about,
 Like withered leaf in gusty autumn day ;
 The mortgage is salvation, but refuse—
 What follows then ? The inadvertent note
 Rises against you, and your doom—a prison.

Wilder. [*Seizing him by the throat.*] Unblushing villain,

Foun. Help ! murder ! help !   [die !

[*Enter* CARRYL.

Carryl. Wherefore this outcry ?

Wilder. [*Releasing his hold, and affecting composure.*]
 Prone to sudden fits,
 Most apt to strike the man whom most I love ;
 Had you not, like a guardian angel, come,
 I might have done a serious harm to Fountain.

Carryl. Not to intrude upon a house of sickness,
 I wandered forth, and, hearing cries for help,
 I hither rushed to offer my assistance.

Wilder. I am attacked at unexpected times.
 A sad infirmity—
 [*To* FOUNTAIN.] I beg your pardon.
 [*To* CARRYL.] I thank you most sincerely ; sir, I do.

Foun. Accept my thanks ; you came most opportunely.
 12

Carryl. Since my assistance is not now required,
  I shall resume my walk.   [*Exit.*

Wilder. O curse my stars !
  Before that wretch to lose my self-control.
  Jove strike him dumb, else his ill-timed report
  May sully my good name at Weeloundell.

Foun. Better be calm—do what I ask to-day ;
  Or tremble for your certain fate to-morrow.

Wilder. I feel suspended by a spider's thread
  A breath may break, and I shall headlong fall
  Down an abyss of infamy and crime.
  If—will the note—the last, be paid ?

Foun. It will.

Wilder. And, instantly I give the cash, destroyed ?

Foun. If from the mortgage—yes.

Wilder. Where are the papers ?

Foun. [*Giving them.*] Nor add, nor alter, nor erase
  one word.

Wilder. Some villains perpetrate unhallowed crimes,
  Devised with cunning to evade the law,
  Yet pray devoutly in expensive pews.
  Such is the world which good men fail to mend.
  Protect that note, or mine a dismal end. [*Exeunt.*

ACT IV.

SCENE I.—*The Boudoir.*

Enter MARY.

Mary. Why does not Wilder come ? He puts me off
With an excuse too weak to be sincere.
If he were guided by an honest motive,
Swift as the eagle he would hither speed ;
But this delay shows apathy or guile.
To her weighed down with misery, like mine,
An hour's suspense seems lengthened to an age.
[*Enter Maid, timidly.*

Maid. Dear me ! Miss Mary, may I come in ? How
can I help you ? Why I would creep upon my
bare knees a dozen miles, to serve so sweet a
mistress.

Mary. I feel your kindness, but it troubles me.

Maid. The folks are 'mazing dubious and down-
hearted ; Mr. Carryl, pale as a ghost, is almost dead
with grief, and does not know where to go, or what
to do.   Just tell me what you would like to have.

Mary. You cannot help me, I would be alone.
[*Exit Maid.*

If, in the revel of unhallowed hours

He blurred my name ; or if, in truant thought
Suspected me of levity or sin,
It is unjust—but freely I forgive.
No more with his bright fancy shall I roam
Amid the hoary past, or wing away
To fairy realms, where love enraptured dwells ;
But, like a pilgrim on a desolate heath,
Without a hope of peace or resting place,
I weary, weary on.
                    [*Enter* CARRYL.

Carryl. There, drowned in tears,
    Unconscious of my presence, she reclines.
    On me they have imposed a delicate task
    Which I would fain forego : what shall I do ?
    Announce myself, or silently retire ?
    I am perplexed—to speak is surely best.
    Miss Mary, I have come. [*Advancing.*]   Mary !
Mary. [*Aside.*] His voice !
Carryl. Pray pardon me : requested by your mother,
    And with your father's sanction, I intrude,
    But if unwelcome, will at once withdraw.
Mary. [*Aside.*] The world for power to speak !
Carryl. They fondly hoped
    You might at my solicitation tell
    The secret of your grief, to them denied.
Mary. [*Aside.*] Tears, answer him.
Carryl. Oh lend a pliant ear—
    Confide in me, and I will find the means

To soothe your sorrow or redress your wrongs.

Mary. [*Aside.*] Truth has flown back to heaven, if he
    is false.

Carryl. Deem not my fervent pleading over-bold ;
    Let me entreat you, for their sake, explain
    What slight or hurt, or unimagined ill,
    Has raised this flood ! O Mary, if you knew
    How sad they feel, how truly I adore,
    I should not meet this silent, cold repulse.

    [*She attempts to look on him, but turns away
        with fresh tears.*

Mary. [*Aside.*] He never wronged me, no ! I am the

Carryl. Have I offended you ?   [wronger.

Mary. [*Impulsively.*] Oh no, no, no !

Carryl. Give me a look, a sign, if not a word,
    That I may guess what wakens our alarm ;
    And I will labor with unceasing toil
    To comfort you. Here, on my knees I pray,
    By love our eyes, not lips, have oft confessed,
    Reveal this mystery : pity your mother—
    Send her, by me, one kind, consoling message ;
    Or go yourself, and chase her gloom away.

Mary. My father's guest should not in vain solicit,
    But I must keep my faith.

Carryl Merely a guest !
    I thought my love deserved a warmer title.

Mary. [*Aside.*] My brain is crazed—I know not what

Carryl. Have I o'erstayed my welcome ?   [I said.

Mary. [*Passionately.*] No, Edward, no!

Carryl. What do I hear?—Edward!
 You never said you loved, but yesterday
 In your bright eye I read, or thought I read
 (Oh idle hope!) a sympathetic feeling,
 And realized the proud, ecstatic dream
 Of suit successful—but to-day, I am
 Hopeless, down-crushed, the wretchedest of men.

Mary. [*Aside.*] Oh words too sweetly sad, to be his
 For we must part—a martyr to my truth— [last.
 True to my oath I sacrifice my life.
 The sooner done, the sooner breaks my heart:
 One struggle, and—
    [*To him.*] Edward, we are to,—oh!

Carryl. Yes, yes, to love. Mercy, speak to me, Mary!
 [*Her utterance fails and she sinks upon the
  sofa: Carryl alarmed is undecided how to
  act. After a pause she recovers.*

Carryl. Joy, she revives! O gracious heaven, thanks,
 thanks!

Mary. If I had sworn to seize the lightning's flash
 And strike him dead, what would that oath avail?
 I could not do it, no, I could not do it;
 My bursting heart, and not my virtue fails.
 Where'er the truth abides, wronged, deeply wronged.

Carryl. What saidst? Again! that I may understand:
 If, unaware, I ever injured you,
 I merit endless pangs; my life too short

To win forgiveness, or deserve your love.

How could I wrong you?

Mary. I have not accused.   [wretch—

Carryl. Who does accuse? Fain would I know the

That look acquits me; sad but blessed smile.

Let me persuade you, to the parlor come

And cheer your mother's heart.

Mary. If she knew all—

Go—say to her, time may do much—leave me!

Carryl. Not with a thought unkind.

Mary. No, Edward, no!

Believe me, oh believe these streaming eyes.

Carryl. Vouchsafe a brighter smile, and bid me hope

Mary. I have but tears to give.

> [*Overpowered she sinks upon the sofa.*

Carryl. Too deep my love, your wish to disobey;

Heaven bless and guard you through each coming

   day.   [*Exit.*

> [*After a pause* MARY *starts up.*

Mary. His words rushed forth, warm from an upright

   heart,

And proved him guiltless: now, I am convinced

That Wilder is the falsest of mankind.

Why did he bind me by an odious oath,

And why send Waters with a specious tale,

If not to hide the coinage of his brain,

For purpose sinister? False forms away;

Rouse woman-firmness—worthy of thy sex—

He shall absolve me or declare the truth,
That heaven's just wrath may on the guilty fall.
          [Enter WATERS.

What, sir, alone ! Does he deny his presence ?
Waters. No, no : if better, he will call to-morrow.
Mary. Return this moment—tell him, sick or well,
    I will not bear his pitiless neglect ;
    That if he come not in two hours at farthest,
    I will, myself, confront him with the friends
    You said detain him.　Instantly depart,
    He knows me, sir ; I will not break my word.
                 [Exit WATERS *overawed.*
    *[*MARY *sinks upon the sofa, and the scene closes.*

SCENE II.—*A Parlor.*

Enter MR. *and* MRS. RIVERS.

Rivers. Again I swear, this is beyond endurance.
Mrs. R. You must have patience.
Rivers. Talk not of patience ;
    I claim the right, a father's right, to know
    Why she so wilfully persists in silence.
Mrs. R. I have besought her, but in vain, to tell :
    My only answer—" *Wait till Wilder comes.*"
Rivers. What wants she with that smiling, smooth-
        tongued fellow,
    And why keeps he away ?　The mystery here,
    Though deeper than the ocean, I will fathom.

Mrs. R. Time and persuasion may, with Wilder's aid,
    Bring us much comfort yet—have faith in him.
Rivers. He shall not interfere with my concerns ;
    I need not his advice—but must assume
    What I have long forborne—authority !
Mrs. R. Have you no feeling for your only child ?
Rivers. Yes, deeply feel, and this my way to show it.
Mrs. R. Wait, I insist, till Carryl does return.
    If he succeeds not, let us both despair.
Rivers. Why should I wait, when strongly I suspect,
    Something has chanced to mortify her pride.
Mrs. R. She has not seen a soul to hurt her feelings.
Rivers. I must be satisfied. Told she the secret ?
                [*Enter* CARRYL.
Carryl. No, sir ; my mission failed.
Mrs. R. How did she look ?
Carryl. I never, Madam, saw a sadder sight.
Rivers. And nothing said to hint her cause of trouble ?
    Nor gave a reason for her mulish silence ?
Carryl. Nothing : emboldened by her tears, I spoke
    In warmer terms than I will here repeat ;
    But my entreaty was of no avail :
    Yet this I gathered, she is deeply wronged.
    And somehow rose the thought of wrong by me :
    And I, too earnestly, perhaps, denied
    I ever wronged her with a word or look.
    I was mistaken ; she did not accuse me. [affront ?
Mrs. R. Where in the world could she meet with
    12*

Rivers. And why sends she so urgently for Wilder,
 And why fails he to come, but Waters sends
 In this clandestine manner ?   That I shall find.
 Hark. hark, his step! Go, call or force him back ;
 He shall not run thus furtively away
 Without a word to us : we have our rights
 Which none shall with impunity infringe.
        [*Exit* CARRYL.

Mrs. R. For mercy's sake treat him with due respect;
 There is a limit no man should o'erstep.

Rivers. Too long have I submitted to your rule.
 Henceforth I shall be master of my house.
    [*Re-enter* CARRYL *with* WATERS.
 Do you deserve our thanks !   Perhaps you thought
 A family like mine. in deep affliction,
 Might deem the truest courtesy is paid
 By coming stealthily and so departing.

Waters. I beg your pardon, I meant no offence.

Rivers. Shall we be judges, sir ?

Waters. Assuredly :
 But judge my motive. and I fear no censure. [sir ?

Rivers. What is your business here ?   Who sent you,

Waters. I bore a civil message to Miss Rivers
 From her friend Wilder.

Rivers. What, sir, was the message ?

Waters. That he. if well. will call to-morrow morning.
 At which, displeased. she forced me to retire,
 And hence I seemed as stealthily departing.

Rivers. How comes it, sir, she was with you offended?
          You do not know! Ay, sir, and so I guess:
          'Tis the dissembler's trick—but let me tell you,
          Without ears I can hear, without eyes see,
          I feel your thoughts—you cannot hoodwink me.
               [JAKE, *who had entered unperceived, now whis-*
                    pers apart to CARRYL.

Mrs. R. Pardon his rage, he knows not what he says;
          When more composed he will make full amends.

Rivers. Return and tell him, in what phrase you choose,
          He must comply without an hour's delay,
          Or I shall tear the reason from his heart.   [well,

Carryl. And add from me that, one who knows him
          If he refuse a sorely stricken father,
          Will force him, sick or dying, to obey.
          This civil mandate—do not think me rude—
          Oblige me, and deliver in these terms.   [answer—

Waters. Amazed, nay stunned, I know not how to
          But—will report your irritating threats.
                              [*Exit* WATERS.

Carryl. Have I, sir, said one syllable too much?

Rivers. No, to the point—my own mind well expressed.

Mrs. R. This angry menace covers me with shame.

Carryl. I know this Wilder, whom you oft have praised.

Rivers. I never praised him, sir, as well she knows.

Carryl. In youth he was a sly, malicious coward,
          Who sought to hide by falsehood his misdeeds.
          —This not the time to enter on details—

He hates me, and would stab me, if he durst ;
I know it well, despite his gracious seeming.

Mrs. R. Oh, changed since then—a good and godly

Carryl. As in the core of certain fruits we trace   [man.
A semblance of the blossom whence they sprung,
So this man's actions prove his tainted source.
(The church gave him no welcome to the world)
Tho' bland his manners, soft and smooth his tongue,
I know him capable of any guile,
To gratify his malice or revenge.

Mrs. R. Oh, say not so, his life belies it all.

Carryl. To him, I fear, Miss Rivers owes her grief.

Mrs. R. No, no indeed, a tried, unselfish friend.

Rivers. What have you seen to warrant this suspicion ?

Carryl. He called to-day ; they were an hour alone.
He thought unseen—straight from their interview,
O'erwhelmed with tears, she rushed into her

Rivers. How learned you this ?   [chamber.

Carryl. Jake saw them, unobserved,
And whispered it this moment in my ear.

Jake. Yees, Massa—shuah.

Rivers. Why told me not before ?

Jake. 'Cause me no tink, Massa.

Carryl. In his attempt
To steal away we fortunately met ;
You entered soon—pretending he had called
To ask Miss Rivers, in his good wife's name,
To sail with her this morning.

Mrs. R. True, he did.

Carryl. A false excuse, her yacht is not in trim.
  Why sought he to conceal his visit here?
  And tho' twice sent for, why keeps he away?

Rivers. The graceless villain!

Carryl. Sir, I do suspect
  That he has wrought upon your daughter's feelings
  By some invention, aimed perhaps 'gainst me,
  But has o'ershot his mark.

Mrs. R. He had no motive
  To wound our daughter or disparage you.

            [JAKE, *looking out of the window.*

Jake. Missus Wilda's coach jes drove up de lawn.

Mrs. R. Most opportunely—say, we are at home.

                  [*Exit* JAKE.

  'Tis kind in her to call: she will resolve
  The cause (if Wilder knows) of Mary's grief.
  In welcome time arrived.

            [*Enter* MRS. WILDER.

Mrs. W. How is Miss Mary?
  I heard she is not well, and could not rest
  Till I called to inquire; what is the matter?

Rivers. It seems you are no wiser than ourselves.

Mrs. W. Bless me! What ails her—is she very ill?

Rivers. Your husband might inform you, if he pleased.

Mrs. W. My husband, sir! Did you say my husband?

Rivers. Certain I did; no disrespect to you.

Mrs. W. [*To Mrs. R.*] What does he mean, and why
    this angry tone ?

Mrs. R. Be not offended, all may yet be well.

Mrs. W. I did not look for this unkind reception.

Mrs. R. Twice have we sent to-day for Mr. Wilder,
    But he comes not—perhaps no time to spare.

Carryl. [*To Rivers.*] The willing heart has always time

Mrs. W. I see it now—an innocent mistake— [to spare.
    A while ago Jake brought him such a message ;
    But suffering with a sudden headache then,
    I sent a good excuse : if we had thought
    His presence was important, sick or well
    He would have hurried in a moment hither. [love.

Carryl. [*To Rivers.*] Easy to find excuse for those we

Rivers. Why came he not himself? Why sent he

Mrs. W. On any business, sir ?   [Waters ?

Rivers. Ask Waters that ;
    If he make no reply, go ask your husband.

Mrs. W. He is abused.

Rivers. No more than he deserves.

Mrs. W. Pray be not troubled ; if my husband knows
    A reason to make Mary sick or sorry,
    I soon shall find it out.

                [*Turning to* CARRYL, *with a smile.*
    Ah ! now, I guess—
    She, on a tender point, desires advice.

Rivers. Well, if my daughter's peace of mind depend
    On the wise counsel of his sager judgment,

He shows vast pity for her *tender* feelings
Twice to deny her wish ; but he is just,
Sincere, devout, with Christian zeal o'erladen,
And when in praying mood may deign to call.

Mrs. R. Oh, you are too severe.

Mrs. W. Severe and cruel—
He may regret this taunt ; I will return
And bring my husband here within the hour,
To scorn your censure and defend his honor.
Forgive my warmth, for this abrupt assault
His wife must needs repel.   When tried and proved
We may forget it and be neighbors still.

Mrs. R. I know not how to look you in the face.

Mrs. W. Much more polite, had this sarcastic speech
Been made before my husband—

Mrs. R. Please forgive.

Mrs. W. We both have cause to weep.

Mrs. R. Do help poor Mary—
But not a word to him ; not you he blames,
Take comfort then, and help us, if you can.

                    [*Exit* MRS. WILDER.

Rivers. Certain, I blame her not—I pity rather,
That one so gay and guileless is allied
To one so vile.

Mrs. R. Condemn him not unheard.

            [*Enter* MARY.

Come kiss me, child.

Rivers. Mary, I am displeased—

No, that is not the word, for I am angry.
You neither trust your father nor your mother,
But send for Wilder, coldly slighting us.

Mary. Deem not my silence, father dear, proceeds
From want of love or gratitude to you ;
But from a high and holy principle,
Which, if I violate, I could not hope
To meet a smile or merit your esteem.
Then, father dear, if you have faith in me,
And love me, as I fondly think you do,
Bear with my seeming lack of confidence ;
And in the time when I may freely speak,
It must be soon—perhaps ere set of sun—
You shall know all. Till then in patience wait.
I am constrained, against my duty bound,
But still I am your own devoted child.

Rivers. Inexplicable ! Yet your appeal I grant
With the best grace I can.

Mrs. R. Dear Mrs. Wilder,   [band ;
Who called just now, has gone to bring her hus-
Be patient then, for all he will explain.

Carryl. Mary ! She hears me not.
          [*Approaching her.*] Mary ; Miss Mary !

Mary. [*Aside.*] He is still here !
And my unkindness has not driven him hence.

Mrs. R. Why do you tremble, child ? Retire with me ;
Excuse us, gentlemen ; be not alarmed.
                    [*Exeunt* Mrs. and Mary Rivers.

Carryl. What have I done to suffer this repulse !

Rivers. If half you say be true no worse man breathes,
But I will not condemn the wretch unheard.
Soon must he come, and shall not, be assured,
Escape my scrutiny.

Carryl. And when you prove,
Grant me the highest honor earth can give,
Choose me the champion of your daughter's wrongs.

[*Exeunt.*

SCENE III.—*A Parlor in* WILDER'S *house.*

Enter WILDER, *agitated: pacing the floor he displaces
some of the furniture.*

Wilder. She signed the deed, not knowing what she
signed,
Nor asked a question ; woman, too much faith.
How else conceal the crime ! Now Fountain swears
The false note will be paid, the mortgage cancelled,
And I once more an independent man.
Auspicious fate ! may no lapse intervene
To mar his plans.

[*Enter* WATERS.

Waters, what pales your cheek ?
Speak man—rejected ? Or, hast won the prize ?
For joy and grief have similar effects.

Waters. Would I had never seen Miss Rivers' face.

Wilder. What is't you mean ? Proposed and not
accepted ?

Waters. I scarce know what to say, or how to say it.

Wilder. Be more collected, man ; be not afraid. [tears,

Waters. While her blue eyes blazed through a flood of
    Her features seemed like marble statue, pale,
    And in the grandeur of despair she stood
    Erect, sublime—a spectacle of woe.
    As if struck dumb, I could not utter word,
    For I was overawed.

Wilder. What, overawed !
    A girl in tears appal a full-grown man !

Waters. Her withering look I never shall forget ;
    With sovereign air she waved me to the door—
    Humbled, ashamed, I bowed myself away.

Wilder. Why you are crazy—this is raving madness :
    No sane or sober man could talk so wildly :
    Come, Waters, tell me calmly what she said.

Waters. You she commanded with imperious tone,
    As subject-like, to visit her in person.

Wilder. What do I hear ! repeat ; said you commanded!

Waters. By Carryl forced before her angry father—
    Treated with insolence—

Wilder. A blunt, rude farmer,
    Whose chief associates are his laboring men ;
    He cannot treat a gentleman politely.
    Quick, tell me what she said.

Waters. Come to your study,
    From listeners safe, and I will all relate.

Wilder. Show its worst front, I wish to hear the worst.

[*Aside.*] And if the worst my fears surmise befall,
Insane shall be the word, and conquer all.

　　　　　　　　　　　　　　[*Exeunt.*

　　　[*After a pause enter a Parlor Maid.*

Maid. O my! How comes this disorder? Sure I fixed
the parlor this morning: dear me, waste brings
want, they say. If mistress finds everything top-
sy-turvy, she will laugh heartily or scold roundly.
There now, things are more to rights.

　　　[*While speaking she arranges the furniture.*

　　　　　　[*Enter a Footman.*

Well, John, what's the hurry? More haste less speed,
you know. Who are you looking for you can't find?

Foot. For Mr. Wilder: where is he?

Maid. Anybody dead?

Foot. Dead or no dead there's much ado somewhere,
and not for nothing neither: just come from Weeloundell—Railroad could not come faster—horses in
a foam, and her ladyship in tears.

Maid. Save us, she in tears! I never saw her sad in a'
my born days. Anybody sick at Weelonndell?

Foot. How should I know!

Maid. Had I been there I would ha' found it out, or it
wadna been the want of asking.

Foot. I saw none of the Rivers' folk: who could I ask?
Stood at the carriage door every precious minit—
Tom sat on the box—out flies her ladyship—off we
drive in a fury. Whew, how we did go!

Maid. All owing to the spots in the sun.

Foot. What do you know about them?

Maid. Didn't I live six months with Mr. Telescopon, the astrologer?

Foot. O yes, I remember—true; and if you are not belied, he discovered spots somewhere else and discharged you without a character.

Maid. You are a very saucy fellow, and I always said so : some footmen, let me tell you, are no better than their neighbors.

Foot. And some parlor maids too : I said maids : do you confess?—I do.

Maid. Hush, for mercy's sake! I hear her coming— let's get out of the way.   [*Exeunt.*

[*Enter* MRS. WILDER.

Mrs. W. Not here! Where is he? Nowhere to be seen,
   And not a soul around to answer me :
   I scarcely speak for sobs, or see for tears.
   My husband, he so gentle, tender, true,
   Who never spoke an angry word, nor hurt
   A mortal's feelings—ne'er trod on a worm :
   Not one on earth could credit what I heard.

[*Re-enter Footman.*

Foot. Madam, Mr. Wilder is in his study.

Mrs. W. Directly go—say I desire to see him :
   Go instantly.   [*Exit Footman.*

[*Enter* WILDER.

Wilder. As quick as thought, I come

As 'twere, dear wife, to anticipate your wish.

Mrs. W. Oh, you have been most grossly vilified—
　　With bitter, biting sarcasm abused,
　　By one—were you to guess a hundred times—
　　You could not hit.

Wilder. But most unjustly, dear.

Mrs. W. I said so, love.

Wilder. You cousin has rehearsed the foul aspersion,
　　Which, from so good a neighbor, I regret.
　　Say, did I ever give you cause to weep,
　　Or ever kept from you a thought ?

Mrs. W. Never :
　　By all you are implicitly believed.

Wilder. Surely I do deserve to be believed,
　　If not, my life has been indeed mis-spent.
　　Some misconception stirs our valued friend
　　To do me this injustice.   Dry your tears—
　　His slurs I will refute.

Mrs. W. I know it, dear ;
　　But rest not under his reproach one hour—
　　Haste, come with me and prove your innocence.

Wilder. Reflect ; would that be wise ?   Hast ever heard
　　There is insanity in the family ?

Mrs. W. I never did.

Wilder. Nor I.   Yet could we trace
　　Some generations back, it might be found ;
　　For mental ills inscrutably skip,
　　And re-appear at unexpected times.

Mrs. W. You do not think old Rivers is insane?

Wilder.   Oh, heaven forbid!   Why am I scandalized?
     Why in my absence, and before my wife,
     Was I, in his unmannered rage, traduced?
     Such rudeness seems to madness near allied.

Mrs. W. Care not for him, but vindicate your honor;
     I am impatient—not a moment lose.

Wilder. What need of haste?   His passion may subside,
     And then repentant he will ask our pardon.

Mrs. W. No peace for me until you stand acquitted,
     And for his insolence he makes full amends.

Wilder. We cannot reason with an angry man.

Mrs. W. My pride, your reputation, call for speed—
     The carriage waits—a promise I have made
     Which, husband dear, you would not have me break.

Wilder. I always yield with pleasure to your wish.

Mrs. W. Now I am happy—find me in the coach.

Wilder. I will just get my hat and gloves and follow.

                              [*Exit* MRS. WILDER.

     I must out-brazen them, else, no escape.
     If half as violent as Waters says,
     I shall lament the sad calamity,
     And, actor-like, feign what I do not feel.
     I hope that hang-down villain is dismissed—
     The only man I am afraid to meet.
     The worst I fear is, Waters' cause is lost,
     So far defeated are my well laid plans.
     Let all else thrive, the less I shall regret.

[*Re-enter Footman.*

Foot. Sir, Mrs, Wilder waits.

Wilder. Say I am ready.

[*Exit Footman.*

Now, like a fearless warrior, to the field
To brave the shock of battle : I am armed
With wit and stratagem—my only weapons.
If cunning ambush start not in my way,
And she prove true, I surely win the day.

[*Exit.*

ACT V.

Scene I.—Before the Village Post Office.

Enter Jake *with newspapers.   1st* Farmer *opposite.*

1st Farm. Well Jake, mail arrived!

Jake. Yees, massa—Train keep time wi' dis yere watch —shuah.

1st Farm. Where got you that monstrous thing?

Jake. Missus gib me Chris'mas.

1st Farm. Silver! Big as a beehive.

Jake. Gxess no, massa; keep time betta' as gold.

1st Farm. What does your master say?

Jake. He no say nuffin—no how.

1st Farm. Has he heard the rumor?

Jake. Dunno rumor; neber see him; know suga-candy, sah, any how.

1st Farm. Heard nothing then?

Jake. Do tell how fellers heern nuffin! Neber heern you say—"dere, Jake:" nobody gib me nuffin, an' suga-candy no come if penny no call, massa.

1st Farm. You are no fool, Jake.

Jake. No, siree—no like some folk—shuah!

1st Farm. Get along, you rogue.

[*Exit* Jake, *with a comical gesture.*

[*Enter* 2*d* FARMER.

2d Farm. Well, what do you think now?

1st Farm. I don't believe a word of it.

2d Farm. But true—Doctor Torrent saw the mortgage lodged for record by a stranger, who paid register's fees—drove to the station in Wilder's carriage; and, they do say, took the up river Train.

1st Farm. What does Doctor Torrent know?

2d Farm. He is a very learned man.

1st Farm. A mere title-page philosopher.

2d Farm. He keeps a dictionary.

1st Farm. Yes, and everlastingly pours out a cataract of big words.

2d Farm. No matter; some people talk aloud to-day what they would not have whispered yesterday.

1st Farm. Whisperers busy themselves too much with other people's affairs.

2d Farm. Maybe so—but something in Wilder's manner I do not like.

1st Farm. Extravagant, no doubt—but he pays his debts. He lives a godly life, has the best pew in the church, the minister esteems him; and the parishioners trust him with uncounted gold.

2d Farm. Why mortgage his wife's farm?—the last thing on earth a husband should pawn.

1st Farm. If true, I warrant he had a good reason for it. But here comes Van Snap. Have you heard the rumor?

19

[*Enter* VAN SNAP.

Van Snap. What rumor ?

1st Farm. That Wilder has mortgaged his wife's farm :
if so, the papers were acknowledged before you, the
only notary hereabouts.

Van Snap. Ask me ! The records will show.

2d Farm. It is the talk of the whole village.

Van Snap. I never listen to idle gossip.

1st Farm. But what is your opinion ?

Van Snap. My opinion ! A counsellor-at-law never
gives an opinion—except in his office.

2d Farm. You know nothing about it, then?

Van Snap. I know nothing till retained.

[*Going, and aside.*

Why trifle with the ignorant, when it don't pay ?

[*Enter* GREENLAKE.

1st Farm. Neighbor, what is the hurry ?

Greenl. I am astounded ! I gave him, a week ago, on
interest, the ten thousand dollars I got for my
north farm.

1st Farm. To whom ?

Greenl. To Wilder.

Van Snap. [*Aside.*] The more fool you. Now, if I can
entice him to my office, I may catch a good client.

Greenl. Tell me, neighbor, is it true ?

1st Farm. No, surely.

2d Farm. Well, true or false, some people have grown

suddenly wise ; and shrugging their shoulders, mutter—" I told you so."

1st Farm. Better consult Van Snap.

Greenl. Counsellor, what have you heard ?

Van Snap. If you are in difficulty or danger, sir, no lawyer in the county is more willing or more able to advise you.

Greenl. What do you think ?

Van Snap. Impossible to think without a retainer—only twenty-five dollars.

Greenl. Did you ever ask anybody over five, before ?

Van Snap. Amount involved large—great responsibility, —but considering you may be a heavy loser, give me five dollars.

Greenl. Am I in danger ?

Van Snap. [*Holding out his hand.*] Always in advance.

1st Farm. Nothing more to be learned here ; we may as well go.   [*Exeunt Farmers.*

Van Snap. Come to my office.

Greenl. No, no ; there is your fee—I am impatient—tell me here.

Van Snap. [*Taking the money offered.*] Now, I can speak professionally. Sir—the farm is mortgaged for forty thousand dollars, a mighty sum : executed before me, a notary public for this county, duly qualified, in presence of my two clerks, according to statute.

Greenl. The farm is his wife's.

Van Snap. Yes—she executed the papers.

Greenl. What did she say ?

Van Snap. Why, laughing, she exclaimed—" Husband
knows all right—hate business "—asked not a question, but signed. Looking at her signature, she,
with a sarcastic grin, blamed the miserable pen
which made her write so badly. Apart from her
husband, she acknowledged the deed, as in such
cases made and provided.

Greenl. I am all in a tremor—get my money.

Van Snap. Bring your proof of debt to my office, and
I will prepare the necessary papers.

Greenl. I will fetch it quickly.

Van Snap. There is need of haste.   [*Exeunt.*

Scene II.—A Parlor at Weeloundell.

Enter Rivers *and* Carryl.

Carryl. Pray be composed : for Wilder soon must come ;
His wife has promised ; she will keep her word.

Rivers. We should have seen the fellow hours ago.

Carryl. He, with a plausible excuse, will try
To blind you with excess of innocence,
Not dreaming what you know.

Rivers. Deep though he be,
Yet I will dive into his rotten heart
And tear the secret out.

    [*Enter* Jake : *hands a newspaper to each.*

Jake. Mail jes arrove.

Carryl. The Evening Post, and only half-past four.

Rivers. While passing here the Express throws out a mail,
　　The Way-train follows in some forty minutes.
　　I well remember when it took a day
　　To reach the city ; now an hour suffices;
　　Amazing changes since I was a boy.

　　[*While he is speaking* CARRYL *unfolds the paper.*

Carryl. "Painful Rumor."—What can it mean ?

Rivers. Pray read.

Carryl. [*Reads.*] "A large operator in Wall Street has
　　absconded ; it is said that a retired gentleman, who
　　resides on the Hudson, below the Highlands, is
　　seriously implicated.

　　　　" Particulars in a later edition."

Rivers. To whom can this refer ?

Carryl. Perhaps to Wilder.

Rivers. Though I detest the man, I do not think
　　He has involved himself in business frauds.

Carryl. Nothing too bad ; judge me severe but just.

　　　　[*Enter* GREENLAKE.

Greenl. I am dumbfounded !

Rivers. Is the house on fire ?

Greenl. For forty thousand dollars it is mortgaged.

Rivers. Tell me, what is mortgaged ?

Greenl. Wilder's homestead.

Rivers. He does not own an acre of the land—
　　Not one ; all by inheritance his wife's.

Greenl. She signed the deed before Van Snap the lawyer.

Rivers. Well, if she did, that need not frighten you.

Greenl. I lodged with him the price of my north farm.

Rivers. I hope you got security sufficient.

Greenl. Simply his note, with interest on demand.

Rivers. The cash is safer in your hands than his.

Carryl. It would be prudent to call in that loan.

Greenl. Am I in danger ?

Rivers. Get your money :

Take no denial—that is my advice.

Greenl. I gave the note to Counsellor Van Snap.

Rivers. Wait not for him ; the law is tedious—hurry.

[*Exit* GREENLAKE.

I care not though he borrow, beg. or steal,

If I had peace at home—but this is news !

Carryl. Might I not from the neighbors find the truth?

Rivers. Like insects fluttering on a forest leaf,

Or midges dancing in the evening sun,

They little heed what rumors are abroad,

If self is not concerned.

Carryl. But such a rumor

Might rouse a curiosity in drones.

Add this to that, it strengthens our suspicions.

Rivers. Well, if you think so—go : but hasten back.

When Wilder comes I may require your presence.

[*Exit* CARRYL.

Something in that man's face I never liked,

Yet could not point to any act dishonest :

Time whispered, wait—the reason will appear ;
And now it looks as it would soon appear.
He needed not for ordinary wants
So large a sum ; but that is his affair,
Which does not trouble me.   Well, time tries all—
       [Enter MRS. RIVERS *and* MARY.

Mary. Order the coach for me, at six precisely.

Rivers. I ask no questions—you shall be obeyed ;
And, as I promised, will in patience wait.
                           [Rings the bell.

Mary. [*Aside.*] If he come not at the appointed hour.
I shall, myself, confront him, with his friends,
And force him to absolve me, or, confess.
       [A servant enters, who, after Rivers has ordered
         the coach, retires.
               [Enter JAKE.

Jake. Massa an' Missus Wilda',   *[Exit.*

Mary. Leave me, father—
Leave me to speak one word alone with Wilder ;
And mother, with my father go—both go.

Mrs. R. We shall receive them with civility,
As it becomes us, and as they deserve.
  [Re-enter JAKE, *showing in* MR. *and* MRS. WILDER.

Mrs. W. This is my husband, ready to disprove
Your base insinuations.

Rivers. [*Bitterly.*] Oh, here at last !
       *[WILDER *offers to shake hands with* RIVERS,
       who refuses.

Wilder. Madam, I turn with confidence to you.
   [MRS. RIVERS *takes his hand.*
 To please my wife, *sans ceremonie,* I come ;
 Neighbors should live in peace, not enmity.
 What have I done to forfeit his respect ?
Mrs. R. Your long delay, and Mary's sore affliction,
 Have moved him to ungovernable rage.
Wilder. Not against me ! If so, most undeserved.
 But is she very ill ?
Mrs. R. There—sadly grieved.
 She waits, impatient to consult with you,
 Not trusting us—console her, if you can.
[*She points to the sofa where* MARY *reclines.* WILDER
 approaches her. MRS. RIVERS *and* MRS. WILDER
 converse apart.
  [RIVERS *paces angrily up and down.* [secure.
Wilder. [*Aside.*] True to her oath—my triumph is
 Obedient to your summons : can I serve you ?
  [MARY *rises, and in a determined undertone.*
Mary. That oath you have so artfully imposed
 Distresses all the house and tortures me ;
 Give me one word, that word, absolved – speak it !
 And spare me from this agony of silence.
Wilder. First let me understand. What is't you mean ?
Mary. Have you a heart—one touch of human pity ?
 Oh, if you had, would you look thus amazed,
 Not at your malice but my misery ?
Wilder. You have my sympathy; I fain would help you,

But fear, in this unsettled state of mind,
It would be labor lost.

Mary. Unfeeling man !

I did believe I had more self-control.

[*In despair she sinks upon the sofa.*

Wilder. I knew not, sir, that she was thus afflicted,
Else at her bidding I had sooner come—
But a physician more than me she needs.

Rivers. We ask not your advice : nor do we want it.
Why has she sent so urgently for you,
And why refuses to confide in us ?
Answer : play not your juggling tricks with me.

Mrs. R. [*To him.*] You cover me with shame.

[*To Wilder.*] Forgive his rage.

Wilder. This hapless state lends her sick fancy wing,
Which far out-soars my guess.   If wish could heal,
Or prayer avail, she soon would be restored
To perfect health of mind.

Rivers. Arch-dissembler !

Wilder. If you forget yourself, permit me, sir,
To claim my due—respect : but all I pardon,
For in her tears your courtesy seems drowned.

Mrs. W. [*To Wilder.*] That I commend.

Rivers. Why weeps she thus ?   You know.

Wilder. Upon my honor I am ignorant.

Rivers. And so you say.

Wilder. I am.   Prefer a charge,
And I will clearly vindicate myself ;

But if you cast insinuations vague,
How can I answer, save in general terms,
And simply say—for who will doubt my word?—
I never consciously did you a wrong.

Rivers. [*To Mary.*] Do you accuse ?

Mary. I dare not—dare not—no !

Wilder. You hear, acquitted ! Are you now convinced ?

Mary. [*To Wilder.*] Retire with me for only forty seconds,
I have ten words to speak with you in private.

Rivers. You heard my daughter, sir ; you are not deaf.

Mrs. W. Do not permit this dictatorial tone.

Wilder. Dear wife, his anger oversteps discretion,
But pray forgive him.

Mrs. R. [*To Rivers.*] Are you mad ?

Rivers. Wife, wife ! I know more than he thinks I know.

Wilder. [*To Mrs. R.*] Some busy whisperer, I fear, has
To win his favor by traducing me.   [sought
[*To R.*] For your own good I caution you, beware
Of arts insidious. It is not my wont
To speak dispraisingly of any one :
But in this case, I say again, beware !

Rivers. Keep caution to yourself. Obey her wish—
Go with her ; and when you return, explain
The secret she tenaciously withholds,
Or I shall find the reason why.

Wilder. Me, sir !
If you suspect that I impose this silence,
I must, dear sir, express sincere regret,

Less for myself than her distracted state.

Mrs. W. My husband never had a thought to hide.

Wilder. I am above disguise ; here, let her tell

Her wildest thoughts—if she in honor speaks.

Rivers. Your looks and words, believe me, are no kin.

Wilder. This, sir, to me is unbecoming language.

Rivers. Some villains in the world.

Wilder. And some rude men.

Mrs. R. In your own house, in presence of his wife,

Do not forget the courtesy you owe.   [passion ?

Mrs. W. Mercy ! What can have roused this burst of

Oh, Mrs. Rivers, you deserve my pity.

Mary. In the next room we must confer alone.

    [WILDER *turns from her.*

Stand all apart, beyond reach of my voice,

For he shall listen, if not elsewhere, here.

Call it a whim, caprice, or what you please,

But stand apart.

Mrs. W. Indulge her freak—I say.

Wilder. And so say I.

Mrs. W. [*To Wilder.*] What fear we though she rave.

Rivers. Well then, as she insists, let us withdraw.

Wilder. Would I might lead her wandering mind aright.

[RIVERS *and the rest retire,* MARY *and* WILDER *advance.*

Mary. Hast in my looks or actions ever seen

A tinge of mental aberration ?   No !

But you have oped the floodgates of my soul,

And passion rushes with impetuous force

To save the true and overwhelm the false.

Wilder. Why am I singled out for this harangue ?
    What have I done ?

Mary. Absolve me from that oath.

Wilder. Sad, sad to see : but how shall I reply ?

Mary. I once esteemed you, thought you upright, pure ;
    But now you stand before me base, deformed ;
    A fiend in human shape, despised, abhorred.

Wilder. Could I restore a healthy state of mind,
    And make you happy, it would be a joy.

Mary. Why was I told, and under oath of silence,
    What you should openly have told my father ?

Wilder. What I have said here, anywhere, is true.

Mary. A base invention all.

Wilder. Well, time will prove.

Mary. Sir, I demand—give me the right to speak.
    Silence is torture ; answer !

Wilder. Thus you repay
    My constant care of your unsullied name.
    Preserve me henceforth from good-natured actions.

Mary. I cannot stoop to crime ; can you ?   You can.
          [Enter CARRYL.
    He enters, see ! Accuse him to his face

Wilder. Like all his tribe, of course he would deny.
    I will not on compulsion prove his guilt.

Mary. A thought, a thought ! I did not think before—
    Poor and bewildered head, how could I think !
    [To him.] I did not swear I never would proclaim

You bound me by an oath—'twas when so sworn,
That I would not divulge the monstrous tale.

Wilder. [*In trepidation, he speaks too loud.*]
You did—and on the brink of perjury stand ;
Forget that oath, and—mercy on your soul.

Rivers. Rushing forward. What did I overhear? An oath!

Omnes. An oath !

Wilder. I know not, friends ; like you, I am amazed.

Mary. A falsehood, sir ; you know I speak the truth.

Mrs. W. Pity, pity ! How long has she been thus ?
Get medical advice ; wait not a moment.

Mrs. R. My heart will break.

Mary. Now listen, father—all !
By cunning, Wilder jarred a tender chord,
Which turned me desperate, yea, to frenzy drove me.
And scarce aware of what I said or did,
He drew from me, deceitfully, an oath—
But what he told until absolved, lies here.
So much, not more, with honor I may tell.

Rivers. Shall I believe my ears ! Good heaven, an oath !
Steal to my house, and like a fiend, entrap
My innocent child to swear, and now pretend
She is insane ! No matter what you told,
It was a lie—a base, malicious lie—
The infernals, surely, are not so profane.

Wilder. If I stood not beneath your honored roof
I might lose patience, and reply in anger ;
But now, in sorrow simply say—not true.

What could have tempted me to such an act ?
Where, when, and in whose presence was she sworn ?
Before what magistrate ?   For no one else
Can legally administer an oath.

Rivers. Swear forty thousand times, her single word,
Thou sanctimonious knave, down weighs them all.

Mrs. W. His truth has never been impeached before :

Carryl. [*To* RIVERS, *who bows assent.*]
May I, sir, ask a question, with your leave?
[*To* WILDER.]   Is this another of your sudden fits ?

Mrs. W. Fits, sir!   What fits ?

Carryl. To which he is so subject.

Mrs. W. He never had a headache—only once—
And I sent Mary our sincere regrets.

Carryl. Some hours ago, by accident we met,
And, in his fury, I saved him from murder.

Wilder. Sir, I disdain reply.   This seems your work :
There is a time—not now—but it will come.

Carryl. And sooner than you think.
[*To* MRS. WILDER.]   Pray, did you, Madam,
Invite Miss Rivers to a sail this morning ?

Mrs. W. I could not, no : our yacht is high and dry,
Under repairs.

Carryl. [*To* MRS. RIVERS.]   In presence of us both,
And [*to* MRS. W.] in your name he did.

Mrs. R. I heard him—true.

Carryl. His word 'gainst hers—you hear !

Mrs. W. [*Slightly agitated.*]   Somewhere some wrong.

Wilder. Misunderstanding merely, which a word
    Would soon remove; but, wife, I will not stoop
    To satisfy their rudeness with that word.
    Let us go home—stay not to be insulted.   [*Going.*

Rivers. Stir not a foot till you confess your guilt.

Wilder. Am I threatened?

Carryl. Deny her farm is mortgaged.

Wilder. Deny, obtruder! Dare not interfere
    With my concerns, not yours: I should deny
    Did that not argue right of yours to question,
    Which, for an instant, I shall not admit.

Mrs. W. What paper was it that I signed to-day?

Wilder. No matter now—at home I will explain.
    [*To Rivers.*] Why am I treated thus? If memory fail;
    Or, if from misconception I appear
    In conflict with her word—I can explain.

Rivers. Nothing on earth more needs an explanation.

Wilder. Without one proof, save her insane conceit,
    I am abused.

Mary. In perfect mind I stand!

Carryl. How many visitors have you at present?

Mrs. W. We are insufferably dull this week,
    And have not seen a soul but Cousin Waters.

Mary. He sent me word, that you had guests at home,
    And could not leave.

Wilder. I sent you no such word.
               [*Enter* WATERS.

Mary. What message did you bring me, first, from Wilder?

Waters. That he had friends at home and could not come.

Mrs. W. Waters, you rave—the world is else stark mad.

Wilder. Baffled, baffled.

[WILDER, *confounded, takes a seat at the table
      and covers his face with his hands.*

Rivers. A weak and paltry shift.

Carryl. Truth safely treads a broad and level path, [ways,
    While falsehood skulks through rough and crooked
    And always insecure.

Mrs. W. [*Going up to* WILDER.] What have you done?
    A wrong? Tell me the worst.   [*He turns away.*

Waters. [*Whispers to* WILDER.] I bring bad news.

Wilder. I am engaged—reserve it till to-morrow.

Waters. [*To* CARRYL.] A moment, if you please.

Carryl. Let it be brief.

[*They converse apart and Exeunt.*

Mrs. W. What do they mean? More ill in store for me.

Wilder. [*To himself.*] Flake, feathery flake on flake,
      unnumbered falls,
    Each in itself of ineffectual power,
    But, in the storm, their aggregation grows
    To Atlas' weight, and breaks the temple down.

Mary. I charge you, by your hope of peace on earth,
    And bliss hereafter, to confess the sin,
    And all I will forgive and all forget;
    Or, if you be a man with human pity,
    Give me, in mercy give me right to prove,
    How much I am aggrieved, or he maligned.

Mrs. W. Oh, husband, kill me not, but say, absolved.

Wilder. [*Aside.*] Would I were on the farthest wave
from shore.

    [*To* MRS. WILDER.] I will not be compelled to
    please her whim;

    But, wife—at your desire, I say—absolved.

    Ask from what crime ?

Mary. That is equivocal !

    I must be sure—again ! From your own lips—

    Speak it aloud—to me—am I absolved ?   [yes.

Wilder. In my own toils ensnared. [*To her.*] Yes, freely

Mary. Freely—and from my oath released ?

Wilder. Released.

Rivers. Now we shall hear the truth.

Mary. Give breathing time.

Rivers. Wretch, I could strangle him.

Mrs. W. A cloud hangs o'er me,

    Dispel it, love, or stab me with a look.

        [*Re-enter* CARRYL *and* WATERS.

Carryl. There is a serious charge preferred against you.

Wilder. [*Rising in alarm.*] What charge ?

Mary. 'Tis I alone should make the charge.

Rivers. Spare not the villain.

Mary. [*To* CARRYL.] You he defamed—

    But I dare not recite the dreadful terms,

    Which cast on us unmerited reproach,

    Nor should you wish to hear.

Carryl. Not if I plead ?

    20

Mary. I shudder at the thought :
  But this I may, with modesty, make known—
  I was compelled, without assigning cause,
  Or suffering you the privilege of reply,
  To treat you with disdain, discard you hence,
  And never look upon your face again.
  I tried my utmost, but my poor heart failed.
  Forgive me—oh ! forgive the cruel wrong.
Carryl. You do not think I ever injured you ?
  That smile confesses it.
Mary. No, Edward ; no !
Carryl. Too base to curse, I leave him to remorse.
Wilder. Allow me just one word—she heard a slander,
  Besought me to conceal it from her father,
  And, if I found it true, to bring the proof :
  It may be true ; I have not yet had time
  To prove it false.
Rivers. Villain !
Mary. Art not afraid
  Almighty wrath will strike thee dumb or dead !
Wilder. The simple truth, though none seem to believe me.
Rivers. Believe! Waste no more time—prefer the charge.
Carryl. Spite against me, I utterly despise,
  Nor ask what prompted it ; but I may guess.
  The arm of public justice is upraised
  To punish your enormous crimes—in one.
Mrs. W. [*Much perturbed.*] What crime ?
Carryl. Sorry that you are present, madam,

But I must speak— 'tis forgery.

Omnes. Forgery !

Wilder. Ha, ha, ha !   And you, sir, my accuser!

    Just what I might expect from such a source.

Carryl. That frantic laugh will not evade the law.

Mrs. W. [*In terror.*] What law ?

Wilder. Who dares defame me ?   You, sir ; you ?

    We met of old, and we shall meet again.

Carryl. In proper place, I trust.

Mrs. R. [*To Mrs. W.*] Oh, do not weep.

Mrs. W. It is not real—a delirious dream,

    Such spectres only terrify our sleep.

Carryl. You are accused of forging Waters' name.

Mrs. W. No, no ; impossible !

Wilder. 'Tis false as hell.

    Why am I charged with a felonious crime

    So easily disproved ?   Waters, deny.

Carryl. Let Waters speak.

Waters. [*To Wilder.*] You know that I refused—

Wilder. In mercy hush, and save me from destruction.

Waters. I was constrained—

Wilder. To brand me as a felon !

    There, be a man, deny ; swear 'tis not forged ;

    'Twill break my dear wife's heart.

Mrs. W. Swear it is false,

    Or never look your cousin in the face.

Wilder. [*To Waters.*] Deny ; do, do—and all I will repay

    By draft at sight upon my banker, Fountain.

Waters. He failed to-day.

Wilder. Who at the dawn foresees
    What may befall ere night records events !

Waters. I could not say the signature was mine,
    Though very like ; for always to my name
    I add a comma, and its want confirmed me ,
    Which I too inconsiderately said.

Wilder. You often sign your name without a comma ;
    Yes, I have seen you do it, forty times.   *
    What is the date ?

Waters. The twentieth of May.

Wilder. On April twentieth you endorsed that note ;
    Clear as the noonday sun—a gross mistake—
    An error in the date—I did not forge.

Carryl. Gave he two notes of similar sum and date ?

Wilder. I will not, sir, be catechised by you.   [*Going.*

Carryl. You cannot go ; the officers of law
    Wait at the door my signal to arrest you.

Wilder. [*Aside.*] No, not one ball to spare ; I dare not
    shoot him.

    [CARRYL *goes to the door and calls the officers.*

Wilder. In thy delicious cup, revenge, there lurks
    A fatal poison seldom found till drained.

            [*Enter two* OFFICERS.

    Am I your prisoner ?

First Officer. If you be Wilder.

Rivers. Seize him ; let not the guilty man escape.

Wilder. I will give bail to answer this foul charge.

First Officer. That you may do before the magistrate.

Wilder. A sudden summons. [*To Rivers.*] Sir, may I
    To the next room, to write a line or two,   [*retire*
    Which were with more convenience penned at home?

Rivers. [*To the officers.*] Allow him; no way to escape.

Wilder. [*Aside.*] Yes, one.

Mrs. W. A century of woe crowds in this hour.
    Oh, must we part! What will become of me?

Mrs. R. Misfortune oft is blessing in disguise.

                    [MRS. WILDER *swoons.*

Wilder. Unjustly charged; yet, earnestly I pray
    That heaven may pardon, as I do, your hate.
    [*To officers.*] I shall not, gentlemen, detain you long.
        [*Approaches his wife, and kisses her.*
    Farewell, dear wife; God bless you, ever—ever!
        [*All flock around* MRS. WILDER.
      [WILDER, *going, pauses at the door.*

Wilder. To-day, to-morrow, or a few years hence,
    It matters not: to all must come the end;
    And, in the grave, like a blind beggar's dog,
    We turn to indistinguishable dust.
    But, solemn thought! the doom in that far realm,
    Where never daylight shines, nor breath respires,
    Appals my soul; and shuddering, I recoil
    From contemplation; yet, in ignorant fear,
    Heaven's mercy trusting more than human pardon,
    I rush, self-willed, to my predestined fate.   [*Exit.*

Mrs. R. Would, as he seemed, he were a better man.

Mrs. W. [*Recovering.*] What have I heard or dreamed ?
   Where is my husband ?

Mrs. R. Be not alarmed ; he shortly will return.

Rivers. Why, daughter, was his crime so long concealed ?
   You should have openly denounced the villain.

Mary. Rather than break his oath, Judea's king
   Gave to a dancing girl a prophet's head.
   Our word once pledged, becomes a sacred bond,
   Which nothing but release, free given, absolves.

Carryl. Or, from a motive we may justify.   [heaven.

Mary. Love, slighting truth, is more of earth than

Carryl. While I admire your eloquent reply—
   Entrapped by fraud—my oath I should have broken.

Mary. Truth came from Him, whence all perfection
   Oh, never let a maid who loves her sex,   [comes !
   And venerates the pure, exalted sphere
   Which she, on earth, is destined to adorn,
   Forget her truth ! 'Tis all we prize or praise,
   For in that word each virtue is expressed.

Carryl. A startling sound.   [*Report of a pistol.*

Rivers. And from my library !

Mrs. W. To which my husband went ! I hear a groan !

Mrs. R. A sportsman in the woods.

Carryl. [*To the officers.*] Look to your prisoner.
       [*Exeunt officers:* CARRYL *and* WATERS *follow.*

Mrs. W. I dread, yet know not what.
           [*Re-enter* CARRYL.

Carryl. Appalling sight !

Mrs. R. Alas! alas! what sight?

Rivers. Speak! hurry! speak!

Carryl. Dead, dead! Wilder is dead.

Mrs. W. [*With a wild shriek.*] My husband dead!

> [*She rushes to the library : the rest for a mo-*
> *ment stand appalled.*

Carryl. His hand has cancelled perfidy and crime;
  'Tis well—perhaps much better as it is:
  For what is life, with truth and honor lost,
  But poisonous water in a sacred vase!

Rivers. Waste not on him a single thought or tear;
  His life one falsehood—piety, pretence;
  But he is gone, and let him rest in peace.

Mrs. R. Amen!

Carryl. His bitter hate of me, dear Mary,
  Caused your distress : he thought we loved : we do,
  And happiness is ours. You will be mine?

> [*She reclines her head on his shoulder, and*
> *looks fondly in his face : he kisses her.*

Rivers. Look, wife! they love. Shall we consent?

Mrs. R. Yes, yes.
  Stay not his asking : be it our free gift.

Rivers. A daughter innocent of guile—a heart
  Still in its newest gloss. I give to thee,
  For thou art worthy. She with faith devout,
  Will worship fondly at so pure a shrine.

Bless mutual love, the sweetest joy of youth !
Then take my child—her richest dower is TRUTH.

[He joins their hands: they embrace.
MR. and MRS. RIVERS, with uplifted hands,
silently bless them.

FINIS.

www.ingramcontent.com/pod-product-compliance
Lightning Source LLC
Chambersburg PA
CBHW032017010726
47493CB00007B/2445